SILENCE

JOSIE JADE

MONTANA SILENCE: RESTING WARRIOR RANCH

Prologue

Mara Greene

JUST A COUPLE MORE THINGS, and I could go get ready. I wanted to make sure everything was done in the lodge before I left for the wedding.

The place had been wedding central for the last couple of weeks, and it was almost clean. If I finished everything up today, then I could spend more time outside this week. And if I had a choice between working inside and outside, I would always choose outside.

Looking at the clock, I saw I had just enough time to finish. I loaded the remaining cups into the dishwasher, put the leftover supplies from making bouquets and centerpieces into a box, and wiped down the countertops.

There was something nice about having a completely clean and reset space. It settled my mind. A twinge of guilt came with the feeling because of *where* it came from, but it was getting better. Slowly.

I grabbed the box of craft supplies and the last of my

cleaning supplies to store in the utility closet. The closet was on my list of things to work on too. I needed to organize it a little better, and the door was getting squeaky.

That squeak sounded loudly when I opened the door—louder than it had been before, and, more than that, it was *familiar*.

The darkness of the closet crashed in around me, and I backed into the corner, making sure the box didn't make any sound before I pulled the door closed.

Quiet.

I had to be quiet-quiet-*quiet*.

If I wasn't quiet, it would hurt. Straps across my shoulders and back. Whispered threats of what was in store for me later. Once it was finished, and once I was theirs.

No, I needed to stay silent. Maybe he wouldn't notice I made a sound, and maybe I could get out of it this once. I'd done everything they asked and everything they wanted.

Who was I kidding? It didn't matter.

It was easier to be quiet and have no voice at all.

If you said nothing, they couldn't punish you for it.

I strained, listening for the telltale creaks of the porch and the heavy, booted footsteps approaching that told me I was no longer safe.

My heart pounded in my ears, and my breath was too loud. I put a hand over my mouth, trying to stifle the sound, but as hard as I tried, a whimper came out when I heard the front door opening.

"Daniel?"

The voice made me blink. That was Emma. Emma from Resting Warrior. Looking for Daniel in the lodge, where I was, crouched on the floor in a closet next to a box of craft supplies.

My knees shook, and I sank to the floor in relief. This wasn't the compound, and I wasn't in danger. The squeaky hinge on the door had sounded *exactly* like the one in my memories.

I was fine.

I smelled the faint remnants of lemon cleaner on my hands and the dust in the air. I heard Emma's footsteps out in the main lodge and her calling Daniel again, telling him they needed to get going to help with setup for the wedding. Reaching out, I touched the wood of the doorframe and felt the fabric of my shirt on my skin.

This was part of the process of grounding myself. It didn't always work, but right now, it was helping.

Standing, I put the cleaner on the shelf and shoved the box into the corner to be dealt with when I organized. I couldn't be in here anymore.

Emma looked over when I came out, startling a little. She was already dressed for the wedding, hands cradling her pregnant stomach. "Oh hey, Mara. I didn't know you were in here."

I forced a smile and nodded, not quite meeting her eyes. For the most part, I was better with talking, but I couldn't right now. My chest was too tight and my throat too raw to make any sound.

Maybe later, I would feel better enough to talk.

Waving to her, I went outside and walked toward home to get ready.

I was safe. I wasn't there. The man my memories made me afraid of was still rotting in jail. He couldn't reach me here, couldn't make me marry every man in that place like he'd wanted. Couldn't make me a shared bride and a toy for anyone he chose.

Women should be seen and used, but not heard.

It was warm, but chills ran over my skin. In my mind, I still heard the sound of a belt marking my skin every time I made a sound he didn't approve of.

After all these years, I hated that he still had this kind of hold on me. But Rayne kept saying that voicing it helped. Allowing it to exist in neutrality took away its power.

Still, the flashbacks had been getting worse lately, and I felt like I was moving backward. Like I was weak because of its ability to hijack my entire mind and body and literally put me on the ground.

But I didn't have time to think about it right now. I had a place to be, and the evil lurking in my mind had no place at my friends' wedding. It had no place anywhere near anyone, including me.

Now I just had to believe it.

Chapter 1

Mara

THE PILE of plates in my arms teetered, and I just managed to keep them from crashing to the floor. That would have been bad. Instead, I got them over to one of the bins for the caterers and released them in relief.

There was still plenty to do, and I turned, observing the tent and the people in it. A variety of glasses were scattered around the space. I could collect the ones people seemed to be done with—it would keep me busy. My mind was still shaky from earlier.

Lena stepped in next to me as I picked up a glass, and she slipped an arm around my shoulder. "Mara?"

I looked at her with an eyebrow raised.

"Honey, you know you're a guest and not the staff, right? You don't have to bus the tables."

A blush rose to my cheeks. "I know." My voice was quiet —so quiet it could barely be heard over the cacophony of voices and music, but I preferred it that way.

If no one could hear me, it was nearly the same as remaining silent.

Lena laughed, but not like she was laughing at me. She would never do that. Lena was one of the kindest people I knew, and my life was filled with kind people. "Do your thing, girl. I just wanted to make sure you knew no one expects that of you here." She squeezed me with the arm around my shoulder. "Just because you clean up at the ranch doesn't mean it's all we think of you."

"Thank you."

I knew it wasn't what they thought, but it was still good to hear it.

Lena jumped and started laughing. Jude had snuck up behind her and pulled her away from me. They were engaged now, but it didn't matter. Everyone considered them married. *They* even considered themselves married. When they did have a wedding, it was going to be a party for the whole town.

Jude spun her around and took her face in his hands, kissing her soundly. After what they'd gone through, and how long they'd waited to be together, they didn't hold back. "Hi," he whispered.

"Hi."

I saw just enough of Lena's face to notice the way her eyes shone and the happiness there. Jude was still smiling when he turned to me. "How are you, Mara?"

Smiling, I nodded. I was okay. It wasn't really the truth, but what was I going to say in the middle of Grant and Cori's wedding reception?

"I was just telling her that she's a guest and not being paid to bus the tables. So I *hope*—" she looked at me with a wink "—that she enjoys herself."

"I will," I said, her joy finally breaking through and making me laugh.

She grinned, leaning into Jude. "Good."

"Dance with me?" Jude murmured in her ear.

Lena flushed pink. "Always."

He pulled her away to the dance floor, and I couldn't help but watch them. They were so in love, and it was clear to everyone in their vicinity.

Grant pulled Cori onto the dance floor as well, and a hush fell over the crowd. The first dance had already happened, and I didn't think there had been a dry eye in the tent. Because there was a time not so long ago when none of us was sure if Grant would be able to stand for a dance. But here he was, the two of them only having eyes for each other, standing tall and without any pain.

In the corner, Evie sat rocking baby Avery. The little girl was passed out entirely, and I smiled. Avery had the entire ranch wrapped around her finger. She was going to have the childhood of a lifetime and struggle like hell when she decided to start dating.

Not far from Evie stood Liam.

My breath went short in my lungs, but this time, it wasn't from fear.

Liam was…

I wasn't sure what he was, but I liked him. I was attracted to him, even though the feeling was strange. He was always kind, stopping to talk to me while I worked and encouraging me to talk too. But never in a way that made me feel uncomfortable.

His gaze swung in my direction, and I looked away before he could catch me staring. Liam was one of the Resting Warrior men. He was brave and bold, not to mention funny. No way would he be interested in someone like me. Most days, I couldn't speak three sentences in a row. And all the stuff in my past? I was broken. Too broken for someone as joyful as Liam.

In spite of all that, I was glad we'd gotten closer lately, grateful to have some kind of connection.

I started gathering dishes again. I knew I didn't have to, but it was simply who I was. Cleaning was what I had been trained to do when I was young and in the cult. It was my job.

All the women's jobs, really. But especially mine. And it may have been twisted, but it was still where I felt the safest. My mind had been trained to view it as a path to safety, and while we were dealing with other aspects of it, Dr. Rayne assured me it was okay. We didn't need to rock the core foundations of who I was.

Yet.

I stacked plates on top of one another until I had a decent pile once more, and I carried them toward the catering area again. These were heavy, but the servers were already overworked. No one had complained when I dropped off the last batch.

CRASH!

My body jerked to the side, the heavy stack of plates nearly pulling me off-balance. Terror ripped through me, darkness pulling at my vision.

No. I couldn't drop another one. Too many this week. I'd already broken three plates, and I didn't want to get beaten again. My body was still in pain, and I shook with it. It was the reason I kept dropping things in the first place, and another beating would only make it worse.

"Mara?" A voice came from my left, and I flinched. The table was right in front of me. Holding plates. I heaved the stack in my arms onto the table, barely making sure they were stable before backing away.

I was present at the reception, but I needed to get out of here and breathe. Too many things, too many smells, and the sounds and voices were overwhelming. I needed something *less* to ground myself.

Beelining for the edge of the tent, I slipped out one of the many entrances into the darkening evening. Immediately, the weight on my chest lifted. Better. Better wasn't even close to *good*, but at least out here, if I lost my shit, no one would be able to see me.

"Mara?"

The same voice I'd just heard call to me inside. A voice I knew.

Liam stood behind me, watching carefully.

Normally, a man following me anywhere would send me straight into a panic. But Liam wasn't just a man. None of the Resting Warrior men would ever hurt me. I knew them well enough to believe that.

The entire point of Resting Warrior was to help people…like me. A safe place for those who suffered from post-traumatic stress, whether that stress came from military service like theirs did or not. They also trained animals to help in therapy, providing therapy dogs, horses, alpacas, and even the occasional cat to practices across the country.

But of all the men on the ranch, Liam was the one I was the most comfortable with. This…attraction I had to him… Was it a crush? More than that? I didn't know. Everything along those lines had been turned against me. Even the feeling of being drawn toward someone else was alien.

He took a few steps closer when I didn't run away. Enough sunlight remained to see him, but what was left of the day was disappearing fast. I wished it weren't—I liked looking at him.

Liam was taller than I was and well-built, though not nearly as bulky as some of the other guys at the ranch. His dark skin caught the last rays of the sun, highlighting cheekbones and a jawline I'd found myself wanting to touch.

"You seemed like you were panicking," he said calmly. "And I wanted to see if you were okay."

I listened to my body. All my muscles were still tense, my heart pounding and my head light. Had I eaten anything? I felt dizzy and jumpy, like things could leap out at me from every corner.

Twice in one day I'd been triggered, and I was...

"No." I shook my head, and my hands fluttered. It was the only word I was able to get out. How did I tell him more than that? There was so *much*, and it was all overwhelming.

It felt like my throat was closing up, and he took another step forward, hand outstretched. "Is compression something that helps you?"

Being wrapped up tight? If only he knew how closely I kept my blankets at night while I slept. Small spaces helped me calm down too. The dark, like the closet I'd hidden in so many times. Somewhere there was a claustrophobic person who thought I was out of my mind.

I nodded once. He'd asked me a question. Yes, compression helped me. And here at the wedding I didn't have many other options unless I wanted to go home.

"Okay," Liam said. "May I touch you? I'd like to help you if I can."

Touch me.

He'd never done that before. And I was almost glad all speech had left me so I wasn't tempted to tell him how *desperately* I wanted him to. And had wanted him to for a while. I knew his offer had nothing to do with me as a person—only with the fact that I was currently in the middle of a meltdown—but I would still take it.

I nodded again, and he smiled. "Okay."

As he stepped in close to me, it felt like so much more than merely helping. Like something momentous, and I wished it were happening differently. But Liam was here, sliding his hands over my shoulders and down my spine, pulling me against him and using his body to hold me.

Compression.

How long had it been since I'd let anyone touch me? More than an arm around my shoulder like Lena had done earlier?

I honestly couldn't remember. No reason for anyone to try. On the ranch, I lived alone, and no part of my job required physical contact with another person.

This was incredible.

It felt like the easiest, most natural thing in the world to slip my arms around him and let him hold me. My face was buried in his dress shirt. He smelled like cedar and a spicy cologne I didn't have a name for.

My heart calmed, and I could suddenly breathe again. The pounding in my ears subsided, and the music and conversation from inside the tent filtered once again into my hearing.

But mostly, I felt *safe*.

In this little bubble with just the two of us, nothing could touch me. Had I felt this way before? Ever?

I didn't think so. Tension melted from my body, some of it I hadn't even been aware of. My legs shook, but it wasn't from fear. It was because my body was exhausted from holding all this inside for so long.

"When I was younger," Liam said quietly, "just a kid, I would wake up with nightmares. Sometimes panic attacks too."

His voice was resonant in his chest, and I couldn't stop myself. I turned my head so my ear rested against him, listening to the steady sound of his heart and the rich, warm tones of his words.

"When that happened, my foster mom would hold me

just like this." He squeezed me gently, a hand moving up and down my spine. "As long as I needed until I felt okay."

I followed his breath, inhaling with him and exhaling too. Long, slow breaths that continued to bring me down and banish the shadows from my mind. But still in his arms, I wasn't sure if it was *calm* that banished the shadows—or just him.

Liam's hand didn't stop moving, drifting to the top of my back before retreating, the movement rhythmic and soothing. "What was it?" he finally asked.

Swallowing, I tried to find my voice. It was there, but it was small. "The dish breaking."

"Yeah," he said. "That can be jarring."

He had no idea.

Well, that wasn't exactly true. No one at Resting Warrior lived or worked at the ranch because their pasts were sunshine and roses. Whatever was in Liam's, I didn't know, just as he didn't know mine. The idea of telling him was at once appealing and so terrifying I flushed despite my face being hidden.

I slowly pulled my face away from his shirt, realizing my hands were grasping the back of it so tightly I was probably making it wrinkle.

Liam's eyes locked with mine, and we were still so close.

So, so close. He hadn't let me go, and I was still holding on to him. The hand that had been moving up my spine was now curled around the back of my neck, and I never wanted him to move it.

"Are you okay?" he asked.

I shook my head. No, I wasn't okay. I probably wouldn't be okay for a long time. But for now… "Better."

He smiled. "Good. I'm glad."

The air between us went tight, and it was too dark now for me to think my eyes weren't playing tricks on me. Liam's eyes hadn't dropped to my lips before looking back at me. I wasn't imagining what it would feel like if he closed that distance. And certainly, the only reason we were still in each other's arms was because he wanted to make sure I was okay.

"Do you think you're okay to go back to the party?"

I pressed my lips together and nodded.

He smiled, and what I could see of it in the darkness made my stomach swoop. "In that case, would you dance with me?"

I nodded before he fully finished the question, though I missed the warmth and strength of his arms as he released me. But he took my hand in his, led me back into the tent, and straight to the dance floor.

Chapter 2

Liam Anderson

GOD, I was so relieved she said yes.

I led Mara onto the dance floor, doubly relieved that the music had slowed in tempo as the evening progressed.

It wasn't *only* because I'd been attracted to Mara for a long time and having her in my arms was a fucking dream come true. It was because of the look on her face.

When she'd run out of the tent, she looked like she was panicking, and I knew all too well what that was like. But when I reached her? It was so much more than that. It was terror. Pure, distilled terror, and I already knew her expression was going to haunt me.

Plenty of things had happened here over the last few years, but this year had been nice and quiet so far. From what I could see, there was no external reason for Mara to be afraid. Every time I'd seen her the last few months, she'd been happy and ready with a smile. Until tonight.

Whatever spooked her came from her own mind, and

god, I wished I could take it from her. I didn't want her to be afraid.

Bringing her around to face me, I pulled her closer and wrapped an arm around her waist again. I liked her this close to me, and I *loved* being able to see her clearly now.

She'd woven her long hair into a crown on the top of her head, and I wanted to unpin it, solely for the purpose of running my hands through it.

Looking down at her hand in mine, I was able to see the tattoos there. They were always a curiosity to me since Mara didn't seem like the kind of woman to get tattoos. And yet, she had several.

A bouquet of watercolor flowers on her hand, along with delicate decorations on her fingers. She also had a tattoo on her back, feathers peeking out of her dress. I'd seen it before as she worked on the ranch. I'd never asked, but my curiosity burned.

"Still doing okay?" I asked.

She nodded. Her hand held mine hard, but I didn't care. Her breathing was easier, and she didn't look afraid.

Daniel and Emma danced close by, Emma's baby bump between them. He looked at me and subtly raised an eyebrow. I checked my reaction, not wanting to alert Mara to the idea that we were attracting attention.

But we were.

A quick glance around the room told me that many, many eyes were on us. Most of them were my Resting Warrior family. Only a couple of them knew what I'd been feeling for Mara, but this was the first time I'd ever shown any public interest. Of course they were going to notice.

Instead of worrying about it, I looked back at Mara. Her blue eyes were clear and fixed on mine. I couldn't tell what she was thinking, and I wasn't sure she would be able to tell me if I asked. However, I refused to believe it had been my imagination when we'd been outside. There was a *moment*, and it had taken every ounce of my willpower not to kiss her.

I still wanted to, but here and now was not the place. While she was in my arms and safe, I was happy. Because I never, *never* wanted to see that look on her face again.

The song faded, and I wished I had the ability to rewind time so I didn't have to let her go.

She still looked at me, and her voice was soft under the music. "Thank you for helping me."

"You don't ever have to thank me for that, Mara. I'll help you any time you need it."

A soft pink blush rose to her cheeks, and I drank in the color. Every detail of her was something I wanted to drink in.

"I think I'm better now, but I'm going to go home."

"I'll walk you out," I said, not fully ready to leave her presence and equally happy I didn't have to say goodbye to her with an interested audience.

She got her small bag from the coat check and found the keys to the ranch truck she'd used to get here. "Are you okay to drive?" I asked.

"Yeah, I'm okay."

The sound of her voice, away from the chaos of the crowd, was beautiful. Lower than you might imagine, and rich. Every word she spoke was precious, and I would love to hear her speak the whole day, every day.

"Have a good night," I told her. "I'll see you soon?"

She nodded, fiddling with her keys as she looked at me. For long moments, the air between us went tight again. I didn't look away. After tonight, I didn't want to hide it anymore. I wasn't in a rush, and if she told me she wasn't interested, then that would be that.

But until then…

"Goodnight, Liam."

She got in the truck, and I watched her drive away. Something about the engine didn't sound quite right. I made a mental note to take a look at it since that truck was the one Mara used most often.

I reentered the reception and went straight to the bar. "A beer, please."

The bartender passed me the bottle, and I took a long sip. I needed some time to breathe. What probably looked like nothing more than a dance on the outside had been the most intense few minutes of my life.

A hand fell on my shoulder, and I jumped. Lucas stood beside me, and he ordered a drink as well. "So?" he asked.

"So what?"

"You and Mara?"

I looked over at him. "You going dad at the prom on me?"

He chuckled. "No, just curious. That's all."

"We both wanted to dance," I said. "So we did."

I wasn't going to tell anyone else she'd had a panic attack. That was her business and her trauma. I was fucking honored that she'd let me help her in such a vulnerable moment. No way in hell I would break that trust.

"Sure it's not more than that?"

Letting a smirk cover my face, I took another sip of beer. "Avery's going to have a hell of a time with you."

"Damn right she is." Lucas looked back at Evie where she stood gently rocking their infant daughter. "If you need anything, let me know."

"I will," I said with a laugh.

Lucas went back to his wife, and a stab of jealousy shot through me, seeing the three of them as a unit. I wanted that. I wanted a family and a home, and I would protect both of those things until my last breath.

"How you doing?" Harlan leaned against the bar.

"Still doing pretty well from when Lucas checked in with me thirty seconds ago. How are you?"

"Is it that transparent?"

Turning, I leaned against the bar too. "No more transparent than all of you staring at us while we danced. I'll tell you the same thing I told Lucas. We wanted to dance, so we did."

"It's just, Mara—"

I raised both my eyebrows. "Is an adult and a friend. That's what you were going to say?"

"Yes, exactly that," he chuckled.

Daniel approached and reached past me for a soda from one of the ice bowls on the bar. "That was interesting."

"You could have been more subtle," I said with a sigh.

He grinned. "Coming from you? The least subtle member of our family?"

"I can be subtle," I said, glad to be on more familiar ground finally. "I have my clothes picked out for next week, and I thought highlighter yellow was a good choice. No?"

They laughed, and I took the chance to escape and stand at the other end of the bar, closer to the edge of the tent. I wasn't quite ready to leave yet, but I was done being interrogated.

Jude walked up the side of the tent toward me, and I rolled my eyes. "Fuck," I said under my breath and took another sip of my drink. "Is it really that bad that I asked a woman to dance? I swear you all are worse than meddling grandmothers."

He held up his hands like he was surrendering. "I get that, but unlike the others, you and I both know it's not just asking her to dance."

It was true. Jude had figured out my attraction to Mara a while ago. Of the guys, he was the one who most understood the situation. "Was this what it was like for you and Lena? Eyes on you all the time like you're in a fishbowl?"

Jude shrugged. "Yes. But I think it's a little different, because neither of us was actually trying to hide our interest. I just had my head up my own ass."

I smiled at that.

"But don't worry about the stares. Everyone here loves you and is rooting for you, and the same for Mara. If you and Mara are meant to be, they'll be rooting for the both of you together. Don't be discouraged by it."

"I'll try not to. I'm just not used to being monitored like there's a spotlight on me. It's not going to make anything easier."

Jude choked on a laugh. "No, it's absolutely not. But you'll still be okay."

"Do me a favor and tell Grant and Noah they can skip coming over to check on me."

"Will do," he smirked. "But don't blame me if it doesn't work."

If everyone thought this was some kind of fling or passing interest, they couldn't be more wrong. I'd started to get to know Mara because I was interested in drawing out the quiet woman I always saw around the ranch. It didn't sit right with me that we had an employee whom I didn't know.

It was her sweet, gentle kindness that pulled me in the rest of the way. She always did more than was required, and she loved to help. Like tonight, gathering dishes at the reception though no one expected her to.

She was stunning, and whenever she chose to speak, my whole being perked up and listened.

I didn't know if I deserved someone like her. But tonight gave me hope. I would never push her or make her uncomfortable. But if she gave me a chance?

No doubt in my mind. I would take it.

Chapter 3

Liam

A TANGLE of rust and dust stared back at me from the truck's engine. I was no mechanic, but I still wanted to look. Working on a ranch meant being around enough machines to know when something was glaringly out of place, even if I didn't know the ins and outs of engines.

Still, the truck had sounded weird last night when Mara left, and when I started it today, it was off. A loud squeaking when it accelerated that shouldn't be there. These things were built to last, and we didn't work them nearly as hard as those who had a traditionally functioning ranch. But this was one of the older trucks, and it was definitely on its last legs.

The crunch of dirt alerted me to a presence, but I didn't move. They'd tell me who they were. Right now, I only saw boots next to the truck, and that didn't give me any kind of clue.

A foot tapped my leg.

I scooted out from beneath the truck just enough to see

that I was surrounded. Lucas, Jude, and Noah were standing there, looking down at me, and all of them looked serious.

Glancing around, I sat up and brushed the dust off my clothes. "You know, I've been expecting this," I said with an exaggerated sigh. "And I'll come clean with you. I *have* been eating the last Deja Brew cookies every week for years without telling anyone. It's okay, I'm ready for my intervention."

Jude snorted. "I knew it was you. And I knew it was you trying to get me to go back to the store early just to see Lena."

I shrugged. No way was I admitting to that, but I also wasn't going to deny it either. The man had needed a push.

Kind of like the one I needed last night.

Shoving the thought away, I looked back at them. "What's up? Provided you're not actually here for an intervention."

"No, we wanted to see if you were ready," Lucas said.

"For?"

"The survey in the back corner for the rehab facility, remember?"

I ran a hand over my face. No, I hadn't remembered. My mind was so caught up in Mara and making sure she was safe that I'd forgotten about it completely. "Wow. I'm sorry. I heard this truck acting up last night, and I wanted to see what was wrong with it. But I don't see anything obvious."

The three of them shared a look I pretended not to see. If they wanted to ask, they could, but until they did, I was going to act like everything was business as usual.

Lucas nodded to the truck. "What does it sound like?"

I hopped into the driver's seat and turned it on, pressing down on the gas so they could hear the squeaking. It was even more obvious when the truck wasn't moving.

He waved a hand, and I killed the engine. "Jeez, yeah.

Sounds like the engine belt is going. Probably a good thing you checked on it."

A broken belt wasn't the most dangerous thing that could happen in a vehicle, but still, the thought of the belt snapping while she was on the road? It hollowed out my gut and made my chest tight.

I focused, letting the thoughts tumble through, one after another. If something happened on the road, the terrified look on her face from last night would reappear. That alone was more than enough reason to fix this truck. Not to mention the possible *actual* danger to her.

I took a breath and stretched, trying to shake the sudden tension out of my body. Mara wasn't *mine*. I didn't own her. I had no more right to protect her than any of the other Resting Warrior guys.

The fierce rejection of those words in my gut nearly put me on the ground. The deep need to protect her made me want to tear things apart—both friendly and not—in order to make sure she was all right.

Lucas looked at me, and I realized the silence had stretched too long. "I'll pick one up tomorrow," I said. "Let's just make sure no one drives this one until then."

"Don't worry," Jude said. "Mara doesn't usually leave the ranch for the first part of the week."

I glared at him, and he just grinned at me.

It wasn't like I could be mad at him. I'd given all of them a hard enough time while they were courting their women that I'd earned everything they might want to throw at me.

"Good to know," I said. "Or anyone else who might use the truck."

Another truck pulled up to the lodge, and Daniel stepped out with a wave before collecting what seemed like a mountain of mail and packages.

"We're headed to the northwest corner, Daniel. Want to come?"

"I do, but I need to take care of some things in the office first. I'll join you when I can." He carried the mail into the lodge, and Jude led the way to his truck so we could head where we needed to go. The back of it was filled with what we'd need.

The location was a good one, but we had to confirm there were no unseen obstacles before we started calling in contractors. And it helped all of us to see something like this laid out in physical space so we got an idea of how big it would be and how it would look.

"How's Avery?" Noah asked. "I saw Evie with her last night, but they stayed out of the action."

Lucas smiled, and you could tell it was an instinctual smile. The kind you couldn't control even if you wanted to. "She's incredible," he said. "It feels like there's something new every day. Hell, I hate leaving the house because I know when I get back there, Evie's going to tell me something she did that I missed."

The little family had taken a month of leave together, and we'd barely seen the three of them in the whole time, but I understood the desire to be present for everything your child did. It was what made Lucas an amazing father and was how I wanted to be when it was my turn.

What I would have given to have a father who was so interested...

"That's good to hear," Noah said, laughing. "Careful, though. Soon, you'll have another one on the way, and things will get even more hectic."

"We do want more," Lucas said. "Not going so far that we're the von Trapp family, but definitely more."

I was the one who laughed this time. "You guys are going to outgrow your house pretty quick."

"Yeah." Lucas was quiet. "I know. It feels strange to even talk about moving off the property, but I think we might have to. Not going anywhere else, just nearby where we could build something bigger."

That I understood too. I'd never lived on Resting Warrior property—by my own choice—for the same reason. But when I came here, I knew I wanted a location I could make a home. One I wouldn't have to leave. So I'd found a place on the edge of town, and for the first few years we were here, I spent every moment I could making it mine.

"Have you told Daniel?" Jude asked.

"Not yet, but I don't think he'll have a problem with it. It's not like I'll be screwing off to go travel the world. I'll just be down the road. Hopefully." Lucas chuckled. "I guess it depends on what we can find."

I tapped him on the arm. "I can help if you need me to. My real estate agent still sends me Christmas cards."

Noah groaned. "Oh my god, I understand that. Do they ever stop?"

"I don't think so." I shook my head. "But she was good to work with and very helpful while trying to find a *property* and not just a house."

"Thanks, Liam. I'll probably take you up on the offer. We're not ready yet, but soon."

None of us was in a rush to chase them out. Things were already wildly different at Resting Warrior compared to when we started, and people moving off the property to raise a family would be more proof things were changing.

A good development, for sure, but there was always a twinge of fear when things changed. Because change could be good, but most of the time, in my experience, it wasn't.

Still, change was part of life, and I was trying to get better at handling it.

Jude pulled up near the potential site and parked the truck. "Everybody out."

"Keep telling me what to do, Mr. Williams, and you'll have to buy me dinner," I said.

He laughed once. "I don't know if Lena would like that, but you're welcome for dinner at our place any time."

"Really?"

Jude frowned. "Yeah, of course." Then he smirked. "Maybe not *after* dinner, when we disappear upstairs. But for the meal."

"Picked a date yet?"

He grabbed the laser plane out of the back of the truck, and I grabbed the stakes and flags we'd need to map out the building. "No," he said. "Not yet. Lena's been so busy with everyone else's weddings, she hasn't even had time to think about it. If I didn't know she wanted a nice wedding, I'd fly her to Vegas tomorrow and marry her."

"At least you'll save money on the catering."

Jude grinned. "Even if she decided she didn't want to lift a finger, I wouldn't care."

A pang in my chest had me looking away for a second. These men were my friends, and I was happy for them. But I wasn't going to pretend it was easy to see them so happy. As the jokester and the prankster here, I knew my role and was comfortable in it. And it had always been that way.

But I found it harder to be the constant lightness now.

Noah spread out the preliminary plans for the building on the tailgate so we could see what the hell we were doing.

"This place is going to be huge," I said.

"Yeah," Noah agreed. "But it'll be incredible."

He was right. The rehab center would allow us to help members of the military who'd been injured and were also struggling with PTSD—like most of us had been. It would take everything we were doing now and push it to the next level.

"We might not be able to do this now," Jude said with a sigh. "I could have sworn this was working, and now the damn thing won't even turn on."

I raised an eyebrow. "Did you charge it? I know older guys like you sometimes have trouble remembering things."

"Smartass," he muttered the word under his breath. "Yeah, the battery was full. Something's going on with the laser."

"Well—" I looked around at the open space in front of us "—I needed to go to the hardware place for the belt, anyway. Drive me back, I'll run into town now, and you guys can still roughly map stuff out, and then we'll finesse it if they have one in stock. I'll order one if they don't."

Lucas put his hands on his hips, and I nearly laughed at the classic "Montana Man" image he was putting off. The only thing keeping it from being genuinely funny was that Lucas didn't have a false bone in his body. That genuineness allowed him to connect with people and animals alike. "It's not ideal, but you're right, Liam. It's better to get it now than wait for it."

We hadn't slated time into the schedule to do this for more than a couple of days.

"Maybe Daniel will be ready to come by the time we get there," Jude said, nodding to the truck.

Noah closed the tailgate, and I saw the two of them look at the plans as Jude and I drove back toward the lodge.

"I hope we didn't come off too strong last night," Jude said.

I smiled but kept my lips tight. "I get it. I do. But I'd like to do this the way we do everything else here. If you see me doing something to self-sabotage or you think I've stepped over a line, then you have every right to step in. But until then—"

"We'll let you handle it," he said.

"Thanks."

Now I just had to figure out if there was anything to handle.

Chapter 4

Mara

I CLOSED the door to the storage shed near the lodge and sighed, leaning back against the surface. Taking stock of all the seeds I had was on my long list of things to do, but my mind wouldn't focus enough for me to do it now.

The whole day, I'd drifted off into thoughts and memories, not able to control it, as if a thick cloud of fog swirled around my brain. Partly from being triggered yesterday, but also with Liam.

Now that it was daylight, and I was far enough away from the experience, embarrassment plagued me. I didn't want him to see me like that. He'd been so great about it, but it was just another strike against me. Mara, the mute. Mara, who was still so haunted, a breaking dish could make her fall apart entirely.

I knew I shouldn't be giving the negative voices in my head so much power, but some days I wasn't strong enough to fight them off. Today was one of those days.

Still, I tried to focus on the good moments too. Like when Liam held me and it felt like everything good in the world. And then we'd danced, and it was…

I couldn't stop thinking about *that* either. How I felt when he pulled me closer, his strong hand around my waist.

When we were dancing, it felt as if nothing in the world could hurt me, no matter how untrue that was.

Shaking my head, I pushed off the door and went to the lodge. The back door was closest. One final thing on my list to cross off before I moved on.

My gut tightened as I approached the closet and the damn squeaky hinge. I hated how much that still had a hold on me, but if I fixed it, at least there wouldn't be any more surprises. Not from this door, at least.

I closed my eyes and opened the door quickly, ignoring the sound of the hinge. Oil and some rags sat on a shelf in here for exactly this purpose. A ranch had all kinds of things that could suddenly become squeaky.

The front door of the lodge opened, and I dropped the bottle, startled. I cursed in my head. This wasn't supposed to be affecting me right now.

Daniel poked his head around the corner of the hallway, holding a pile of mail that was far too tall. "Oh hey, Mara." He smiled. "Good to see you."

I held up a hand in greeting. There was no voice to be found in my throat right now. Finally, a few minutes later, the door swung with no sound at all, and something eased in my chest.

Upstairs, gentle creaking told me Daniel moved around in his office. Through the windows, I heard birds and the brush of wind against the walls. I smelled the scents of oil and grease from the rags, along with spilled coffee from earlier this morning. I felt the texture of the rag under my fingers, rough and worn, and the floor pressed up into my feet.

The little things I grasped for weren't much, but they were enough to ground me. I was here at Resting Warrior, and I was safe. The source of my distress was gone, and I needed to breathe.

A small part of me wished I could go to Liam and let him hold me all over again, just like yesterday. That kind of safety? I could get addicted to the feeling. One hit and I already craved more. But I couldn't. I didn't even know where he was, and I didn't want to use him like that. He deserved better than to be a broken woman's emotional crutch.

I put the oil and rags back where they belonged, wiping the remaining grease off my hands. My breathing was easier, and I felt more clarity. I needed to do things today without interruption. Now I just hoped I could actually complete them.

The ranch had new clients coming in later this week, and I had to make sure the cabins were clean and stocked with both linens and the nonperishable foods we provided. The perishable ones, I'd grab the day before they arrived, but I needed to make a list of what we already had, probably do a few loads of laundry, and run into town to the grocery store.

My steps were lighter as I went into the main room and grabbed the notepad I used to make my lists. Last time I'd visited the Bitterroot Cabin, I was pretty sure I'd seen it was out of pasta—

"Mara?"

I looked up to find Daniel on the stairs. I hadn't even heard him come down them, which was a sure sign I was feeling better. The Resting Warrior men tended to be more silent because of their training, but I nearly always heard them.

Daniel didn't look happy. Not angry either, just…troubled. "Come up to the office for a second? You got a piece of mail, and it's a bit strange."

My eyebrows rose. Weird. I didn't get mail. The very small amounts I did get were the standard junk mail sent to anyone with a pulse. I didn't sign up for much, and my name wasn't on anything official when it came to Resting Warrior. Most everything I did was via email, but even that…I didn't do often.

I followed Daniel up to the office. It was getting a little out of hand, stacks of paper on his desk and piles of mail. I made a note to come in here and do some dusting the next time he left the lodge. The man probably wouldn't care if there was a hole in the roof while he worked, but it was my job to keep the place clean, and I was going to do it.

"One of the boxes I picked up at the post office today. It didn't have your name on it, just the Resting Warrior main address, but when I opened it—" he shrugged "—seems pretty clear that it's for you. Is everything all right?"

He gestured to a box sitting on one of the chairs, and I frowned. It was a relatively small square box and nothing I immediately recognized. Had I ordered something? On super-rare occasions I ordered something online and had it delivered, but I couldn't remember doing so recently.

The flaps had dropped shut, and I pulled them open.

I froze.

A pile of white silk lay in the box. Shapes were embroidered on the thin, sheer fabric. Flowers and smaller symbols I didn't want to remember. Things that represented a man—and a group of men—I never wanted to think about again.

I reached out and picked up the pile of fabric. My hands didn't feel like my hands at the moment. They belonged to someone else, someone who was only moving because she had to.

The thin band went around your forehead…

Bile burned low in my throat, sickness threatening. I would know this veil anywhere, because I'd seen it every day for almost a year. Embroidery like this took time, and I'd done everything in my power to make it take longer. All the women in the cult were tasked with making the dress and veil for the brides of honor. The woman—

The girl. Not one of them had been a woman. The girl was chosen to marry him and, by extension, every man in the compound. To be shared however they wished.

It was an *honor*. They insisted. Only the best and the purest were chosen, and when the dress and veil were complete, the marriage was formed. The only piece of color on the frothy confection of fabric was my name, sewn in red on the inside of it.

I looked at Daniel, and he was studying me with concern. What did he think this was? They didn't know. Not about this. What would they think of me when they knew what I'd been chosen for? What kind of person makes it seem like she's perfect to be married to twenty men? Was that how many there were? More? I couldn't remember.

Whatever peace I'd found in the last few minutes was gone. I needed to go. I needed to be away from here. And I couldn't tell Daniel about this. I needed—

My thoughts ground to a stop again. Where did this come from? He was in jail. *Malcolm was in jail.* Wasn't he?

Icy dread poured over me like someone had dumped the entire body of Flathead Lake on my head. I tossed the veil back into the box and shut the top like it was a live snake I was trying to contain. "I—"

Only tightness in my chest. Speaking felt like unleashing poison. But he had to let me go. "Need to go."

"Mara, if you need help—"

I snatched the box. "Rayne," I managed the name before

I grabbed the box and sprinted for the stairs. Even the therapist who partnered with the ranch didn't know everything, but she knew enough to understand. I just had to get to her.

"Mara." Daniel's voice called behind me, and I shook my head. I couldn't stop. If I stopped, it would all catch up to me, and I wasn't sure I could handle it.

Who was I kidding? I wasn't handling it. At all.

"Mara." Daniel's voice was firm, and I looked over my shoulder. He wasn't following me. "Take a different truck than normal, please. The guys were working on the one you prefer this morning."

I blinked. That wasn't what I thought he'd say. I was sure he'd call me back and demand to know why the hell a wedding veil had shown up at the ranch with my name sewn into it. But he just nodded when I chose a different set of keys. "Be careful."

Careful.

Nodding, I pushed out the front door and down the steps to the truck, tossing the box on the bench seat and making it slide as far away from me as it could be without falling out the other side.

Apparently careful was what I hadn't been, if the veil was showing up here. But more than that, was he out? It was all I could think about. Did they let him go without telling me? They wouldn't do that, right? The man was in jail for a sex crime. With minors. It had been nearly twelve years since the conviction, which meant he was supposed to be in jail for another twenty-three.

Not a day went by that I didn't think about the number and feel relieved by it.

The thought that he could be out and sending me this? Another wave of sickness flooded my stomach and chest, and I just managed to hold it back. I kept myself on the road, following traffic laws, but barely.

It didn't matter if Rayne had clients. I would wait. As long as it took until she could talk to me. If I could manage to get a word out at all.

A ring had wrapped itself around my throat like a hand squeezing. It stole my breath and my voice, and it wanted to take so much more from me. My safety and my happiness. My peace. The life I'd found.

Because that was the thing about brides of honor. Once you were chosen, it was for life. It didn't matter how long the dress and veil took to complete, you belonged to them even if they couldn't touch you yet.

If you ran away or tried anything else, like ruining the dress or getting someone else in the commune—or worse, someone outside of it—to want you or defile you so you wouldn't be good enough, you were still theirs. They would just punish you.

I'd seen it more than once.

I flinched at the images flashing behind my eyes. Things I tried to forget and things I'd worked through with Rayne, but they rose like a tide through the barriers I'd erected, threatening to drown me. The bruises and the cuts, along with the blissful smiles of the brides in pain. Because she deserved it, and now that she'd paid her punishment, she was once again worthy.

Until they said she wasn't and it started all over again.

I parked the truck in front of Rayne's little house-turned-office on Main Street in Garnet Bend. Even from the outside, it was cozy, and I appreciated it. If the office had been in something like an office building or tucked into one of those little retail stores next to a dry cleaner, I wouldn't have made it through the door.

Probably plenty of clients who came here felt the same way. With the judgment some people cast on therapy, it was hard enough to make yourself go, let alone go and feel like you were going into a store and picking up a solution off the shelf.

One box of therapy, please. Will that fix me? How long does it take to work?

If only it were so simple.

The world would be a better place if it were.

But the world wasn't a good place. I knew that better than anyone. Montana might be the last best place, but outside of the ranch and the people who'd become my family? I shuddered. Bad people lived everywhere.

My hands shook as I leaned across the seat and grabbed the box. It was like forcing myself to reach out and grab a red-hot poker.

The front office was empty, as it usually was. Rayne had a front desk but no receptionist. The desk was more a place for her to keep the schedule and patient records than anything else.

Her office door stood open, but that didn't mean she was free. The front door closed behind me, and her voice floated out. "Hello?"

Come on, Mara. Talk. This is the place where you need to be able to.

But my voice stuck in my throat like it was trying to force itself through an opening too small to fit.

Rayne's footsteps sounded. "Hello? Oh, Mara." She did a double take when she saw me. "Mara, are you all right?"

I shook my head. No, I was very much not all right.

"Come in, please."

Hauling in a deep breath, I forced one word, painful as it was. "Sorry."

"Don't be sorry. You came at the perfect time. And you know me, I don't believe in coincidences. Would you like some tea? Or some hot chocolate?"

Something we did in our sessions—a ritual to ground me

each time I visited. Similar to how I looked around and chose the things I heard, saw, felt, and smelled. The ritual reminded my subconscious I was here and safe. "Tea."

"All right."

I sat in the chair I used and didn't move. The box rested on my lap. I didn't want it there, but I also didn't want it anywhere else, because as strange as it sounded, I wanted to see it. I needed to make sure it stayed where it was—like it was a dangerous animal I needed to keep in my line of sight.

"What's in the box?"

"My—mm." Pressing my lips together, I gripped the box tighter. Of fucking course. I was so messed up over all this that even in the place I was supposed to feel safe, I wasn't going to be able to talk about it.

"Mara," Rayne said, setting a mug of water and a tea bag on the low table in front of me. "I'd like you to do three rounds of square breathing with me, all right?"

Right. I inhaled for a count of eight and held it for the same, breathed out for eight and held it. Again, and a third time. These were all things I knew how to do and had done countless times by now, and still, I needed to be reminded.

Shame washed up over me, even though I rationally knew it had no place.

I looked up and met Rayne's eyes. She smiled gently. "You're okay," she said. "You're here, and nothing in this office will hurt you. Do you still believe that?"

Slowly, I inhaled. Exhaled. "Yes."

"I'm glad to hear it. Take as much time as you need, but I'd like to know what's in the box since it seems like it's the thing that brought you here."

"Can you look at it?" I asked.

"If you'd like me to."

I handed her the box, my hands clearly shaking as I passed it over. She opened the box, and it was a small miracle to see she wasn't afraid of it. Her brow furrowed when she pulled the pile of frothy fabric out into the air.

She looked at me. "From what you've told me, I know you're not recently engaged. This is from your past?"

I nodded. There was more I hadn't told her about it, and I pushed the words out, every sound of my voice in the silence relieving some of the pressure in my chest, even if the words were halting.

The brides of honor and what it meant to be one. The real truth of why everything had happened. Why I sat here with her now. But I still didn't know *why* or *how* that thing was here.

Rayne nodded slowly, carefully folding up the veil and putting it back in the box. She set it on the table between us. "Thank you for telling me all of that, Mara. I know it wasn't easy. And you're probably feeling a bit raw right now."

I blew out a breath. "Yes."

"And you think this means he's out of prison?"

"What else could it mean? He's the only one who would want to send me something like that. To terrorize me."

She looked at me carefully. "Not any of the other men you mentioned?"

"They disbanded The Family," I said, swallowing but not feeling much conviction behind the statement.

Rayne nodded. "Tell you what, let's call and find out if he's still in prison. No point in worrying about something if we don't know if it's a yes or a no, right?"

I blinked. "You can do that?"

"If you know where he is, yes."

For sure, I did. Moving to her desk, I gave Rayne the information for his prison down in Phoenix. In no more than a minute, she had the general information number. "Write down his name for me."

She knew his name—I'd mentioned it enough times. But

in this case, I was glad she didn't take the chance of getting it wrong. Still, writing his name on the notepad felt like I was sticking my hand into mud.

Malcolm Novic

Rayne flipped the phone to speaker. "Hello, I'm calling to check on the status of an inmate."

"Name?" the male voice answered, sounding bored.

"Malcolm Novic."

The man didn't even hesitate. "He's here, and he's fine. But if you're calling about the parole hearing, I'll tell you, *again*, that's not this number. It's—"

I didn't hear the rest of whatever he said. The rushing sound in my ears drowned out the words.

Parole hearing.

Somehow I ended up back in my chair across the room, knees pulled up to my chest. He was still in jail, but there was a chance he wouldn't be. Panic welled up in my throat, and I couldn't force it down. My soul was a hurricane trapped in the statue of my body. What would I do?

Did that mean he *was* the one who sent me this? Was it a threat? I didn't know, and I didn't understand. All I knew was that this place I'd come to feel like home no longer felt safe.

"What's the reason he's up for parole?" Rayne asked.

"Good behavior."

Sickness roiled in my gut. Good behavior. How could any kind of good behavior make up for what he'd done? To all those women?

"Thank you."

Rayne ended the call and came over to me, crouching by my chair. For a few minutes, I stared into space, but the quiet peace of her office and her steady presence brought me down.

I finally looked over at her, and she nodded. "You okay?"

"No," I said.

She smiled. "Yeah, I don't think I would be either. Well, he's still in jail. As for who sent the box, I'm not sure. There are some possibilities, and we'll talk about how to track them down. The first option would be to ask your lawyer. If you need me to help you with an email or call, I can do that later this week."

Later this week. At our regular appointment. I jumped out of the chair. How long had I been here, taking up time that wasn't mine? How long had I been away from the ranch when I had work to do? "I'm sorry," I whispered. "I took up so much time."

"Mara, you're never a bother, and I'm always happy to help you. You don't have to go through things like this alone. I'm glad you came to see me."

"Yeah." I grabbed the box from where it sat on the table, not sure what I was going to do with it. Part of me wanted to light a fire in the lodge and burn it, and another, greater part of me knew I couldn't do that. We might need it for evidence. Regardless, it would be a splinter in the back of my mind wherever I kept it.

"It'll be all right, Mara. I promise. I'll see you soon, okay?"

"Okay." I beelined for the door, barely even comprehending when it opened, and someone was there. I didn't have enough time to stop, and we crashed together. The box slipped out of my hand and rolled onto the sidewalk.

Thankfully, the veil stayed inside it instead of falling out and blowing away, never to be seen again.

I tried not to be disappointed.

"Oh my god, I'm sorry," the person said. "That was entirely my fault."

"Hello, Brynn," Rayne said. "I don't have you down until tomorrow. Is everything okay?"

"Really? *Shit*." She swore under her breath. "I'm sorry, I'm a mess. And I ran into…" She paused, and I looked up at her. She was around my age, with dark hair and a friendly smile. I wasn't really in the mood to make friends, but if I was going to run into her here at Rayne's office, I had to be polite. "Mara."

"Mara. I'm really sorry, Mara. Are you all right?"

Nodding, I lunged for the box on the sidewalk and didn't stop until I was back inside the truck, the box in its spot across the seat.

Rayne might say it would be fine, but it didn't feel that way. I needed to make it better, and since I was in town, I'd make the stops I needed on the way so I could go home and not leave for a good long while.

Chapter 5

Liam

THE GARNET BEND hardware store was a mix of one of those big box stores and the messy, overfilled, and overpriced mom-and-pop stores you saw in every movie. Big enough to get almost whatever you needed, which was good, considering the number of ranchers in the area with various repairs and construction projects. But it also had the small-town feel that made this place feel special.

However, today of all days, it wasn't looking like they had what I needed. Which was unfortunate, because having to order it would put us behind a few days. But at the same time, we didn't have a hard deadline on the building, so no one was going to be devastated.

"Jeff," I called, coming up to the counter.

"Liam," he said with a laugh, bracing himself on the counter. "What can I help you with?"

"I'm hoping you're going to tell me you have a laser

plane hidden in here somewhere I'm not seeing and that I don't actually have to order one."

He winced. "I wish I could tell you that, but it's not true. Sold the one I had a few days ago to some contractors out of Seeley Lake. Got another one on order. But if you're going to need one, might as well tack on another."

"Yeah," I sighed. "Ours out at the ranch seems to be busted. Not exactly sure why, but we're blaming Jude for it."

Jeff chuckled. "Well, you've got some different options. We can go through them."

Out of the corner of my eye, I spotted a figure I'd know anywhere. But what was Mara doing here? "Give me a second," I said. "Pull them up? I'll be right back."

I ducked down the aisle, looking around until I saw her, arms full and loading things into a cart. "Mara?"

She looked up, startled, and then visibly relaxed when she saw me. Still, her eyes slid past me and back to her cart.

After yesterday and this morning, she wasn't far from my thoughts. And with her standing in front of me right now, I was struggling to keep those thoughts in line.

Mara's wild hair was long, loose, and hid her face as she picked another…security camera off the shelf and put it in the cart. One glance showed me she had several.

If she was here on an errand from Daniel, it wasn't all that strange. But still, she seemed more skittish than normal. "I didn't expect to see you here, of all places."

"Yeah." Her voice was quiet, but clear. "I just needed some things."

She looked quickly up at me and then back down.

I cleared my throat. "Are you…" Her tone was throwing my instincts off, and after yesterday, I wasn't sure where we stood or what was appropriate. "Are you all right? After yesterday."

She turned and pulled some extension cords off the shelf,

adding them to the cart with the cameras. No response came from her. "Mara?"

Freezing for a second, she shook her head. "Fine. I'm fine."

I swallowed, fear compressing my chest. Trying to shove it aside, I cleared my throat. "The truck you use on the ranch. There's something up with the engine belt in it. One of the reasons I'm here, actually."

Mara straightened, throwing the last of her selections into the cart. "Daniel" —her voice was soft— "told me to take another one."

She pushed the cart down the aisle right by me, and I got a breath of her gentle fragrance. Floral, like daisies, fresh and sweet. It hit me nearly as hard as the fact that she was basically ignoring me.

"It's fine. Don't worry about it. You're worrying too much, Liam. Why do you always need so much?"

The words echoed in my head in a voice that was distinctly not Mara's. I knew better than to assume Mara's silence had anything to do with me, and yet I couldn't erase the gnawing in my gut telling me I'd experienced this before. That I'd given away some part of myself to someone who didn't really care and was only in it for motives I couldn't count on.

I shook my head. Jeez, Liam. Get your head in the game.

Following her up to the front, I kept my distance so she didn't feel like I was crowding her as she checked out with Jeff. Security cameras, extension cords, and what looked like a coded deadbolt lock. She kept glancing over her shoulder but not at me. Toward the plate-glass windows and doors and the parking lot outside.

Like she was afraid the windows were going to explode inward.

She was scrambling to get out of here quickly, and she

was shaking. It wasn't uncommon. I'd seen her shake before around the ranch, and given yesterday, it made sense she was jumpy. Still, something else felt wrong.

"I'll see you later, Mara?" I asked as she was pushing her cart out the door.

She glanced behind her once, and her face was blank. Not terrified or devastated, just blank. Nodding once, she turned and left. I tried not to let it feel like a punch to the gut, but it did.

What I wanted was to follow her and turn her around. Get her to *look* at me and tell me what was happening and if she was okay. Because she didn't look okay. And yet, Mara wasn't mine. As much as I wanted her to be, she wasn't. I had no right to know about her emotions and thoughts, even after supporting her in a vulnerable moment.

"You ready?" Jeff asked, gesturing to the computer, where the details of the laser planes were up.

"Yeah." I dragged my eyes away from Mara and looked at the screen, managing to focus long enough to order what we needed and put it on the ranch's account. I grabbed the belt for the truck as well before heading out, but I couldn't go straight back.

As fucked up as it might be, if I went straight back to the ranch, I wasn't sure I could stop myself from going to Mara's house and asking her if she was all right. Or wherever she was on the ranch. I needed to get myself together.

No better place to do that in town than Deja Brew.

After driving over, I scrubbed my hands over my face before I jumped out of the truck and went inside.

"Hey!" Lena was beaming when I went in. "Look who else stopped in today."

She pointed, and I followed her finger to see Harlan sitting in one of the chairs with a cup of coffee. He lifted it in my direction. "I'm waiting for Grace."

"Excellent. Thought I'd grab some coffee before heading back to the ranch. Care if I join you?"

"Sure."

Lena passed me a cup, and I sat down on the couch with a sigh.

"I thought you guys would still be out there," Harlan said.

"Well, the laser plane died, so I came to see if we could get a new one. And a belt for one of the trucks. Was gonna come in for that tomorrow anyway, so I decided to play errand boy."

Harlan chuckled. "Well, at least you get coffee out of it."

"True." I looked at him. "Is this where you always are? Sitting on your ass while we toil away?"

Nothing about my tone said I was serious, and he laughed. "Yeah," Harlan said. "This is where I am. I've secretly quit, and I spend all my time hiding out so the rest of you can do the hard work."

"Your secret is out. Can't hide from me now." I took a sip of the coffee and glanced out the windows. She was probably long gone, but I still hoped to see Mara drive by.

"You okay?"

I looked back at Harlan. "Yeah, why?"

He shrugged. "Don't know. Just seem off."

"Is this where you confess your undying love for me, Harlan?" I placed my hand over my heart. "You know, I've always sensed this chemistry between us. I know you have Grace, but I think it's time we explore it."

He nearly choked on his coffee because of the sudden laughter, and I grinned, taking a sip of my own drink. The guys knew I was rarely serious, and it was true. I liked messing with them.

But it was also a good way to change the subject when I needed to, like I did now. Everyone was already interested in me and Mara, and until I knew better where we stood, I wanted the grace of anonymity.

The chime over the door sounded, and Grace entered.

Harlan stood, eyes only for his wife. The two of them had been through hell, and watching the tenderness they had for each other now raised the same feelings I'd had at the wedding last night. An ache and a desire I wanted desperately to fill.

Standing, I clapped him on the back as I passed. "I'll see you later, Harlan. Grace."

I needed to get back anyway and tell the other guys about the delay. And maybe the short drive home would let me get my head on straight.

Chapter 6

Liam

THREE DAYS since the hardware store. Three days of slowly retracing the same thought circles in my head, over and over again, wondering if I should go see Mara and, at the same time, not wanting to push too hard.

But the thing truly driving me mad was I hadn't seen her. Not even in passing. I couldn't remember a time in the last three years when I'd gone more than two days without running into Mara, even if it was only seeing her in the distance as she went around doing things on the ranch.

Three days? It felt like an eternity, and my instincts were *screaming*.

If I didn't do something, I was going to lose it.

I knocked on the door frame to the office, and Daniel looked up. He had reading glasses perched on the tip of his nose, and I smiled. He was looking more and more like a father by the day. "Hey, Liam. What's up?"

"I was just wondering if you've seen Mara. It's been a few days, and I haven't even run into her. Seems a little odd."

The man smiled but didn't make a comment about why I was asking. I appreciated that, at least. "No, I haven't. But I didn't expect to either."

"Why not?"

Daniel shrugged. "She asked for a few days off, and she never asks for vacation. I think she more than deserved a break."

"Was this before or after you sent her to town to buy the cameras?"

"What?" He was looking down at his computer screen, not fully focused.

I crossed my arms. "I saw her in town at the hardware store, buying a bunch of security cameras. I assumed you sent her to buy them."

Daniel blinked and frowned, now focusing on me. "No, I never did that."

All the instincts I'd been desperately trying to ignore since the wedding came racing to the surface. The way she was terrified and triggered. Then buying security cameras, along with being jumpy? If I was overstepping my boundaries, then I would accept my fate. But I wasn't just going to sit on the sideline if Mara was in trouble.

I turned, and Daniel's voice pinned me to the spot. "Is there something I should know, Liam?"

"Is there something *I* should know?" I challenged him.

The look on his face told me everything. There was something he couldn't tell me, because it wasn't his information to give. "You don't have to tell me to be careful," I said, leveling my gaze at him. "I will be. But don't tell me to stay here."

He nodded. "I won't. Let me know if you need something."

I heard the truth of his words. If there was something deeper to this, he needed to know. "Take no chances" had become the motto of the ranch in recent years.

I jumped in my truck and drove to Mara's house. We all knew where it was, in a corner of the ranch, tucked away. But I'd never been there. As far as I knew, most everyone in our little family hadn't. We wanted to allow her privacy.

The small cabin was one story, and it was exactly the kind of place I imagined Mara living. I smiled in spite of myself. Given that it was late summer, not many flowers were left, but this place would be beautiful in the spring and early summer.

Ivy and flowering vines crawled up the side of the house, and huge flower beds surrounded all the walls, along with more patches lining the path up to the door. The house being on an angle, I could see a more practical garden in the back.

No truck here. She tended to leave them up at the lodge and walk most of the way. But I hadn't realized how far away this corner was. If she wanted to use the truck, she could. But Mara never took anything that wasn't absolutely necessary.

I turned off the truck and stared at the house. My whole body tingled with a strange combination of relief and nerves. Relief from finally following what my instincts had been telling me to do for days, nerves because I didn't know what I was about to find.

But I couldn't wait anymore.

The cameras she'd bought were up on the edges of the house. They weren't secured well. One looked like it was hanging on by a thread. It was clear she'd put them up as quickly as she could before retreating. What I wanted to know was *why*?

I knocked on the door. "Mara?"

It didn't take long for her to answer. She likely heard the truck pull up and knew someone was here. It also didn't take long for me to know that something *was* wrong.

Mara was pale, and she wasn't looking at me. She wore leggings and a camisole that showed more of her than I'd ever seen, but the way she curled in on herself, hiding... I hated it.

She took a step back and gestured for me to come in without saying anything.

"I'm sorry," I said after she closed the door, "if I'm interrupting your vacation and you want to be left alone. But I hadn't seen you, and with the wedding and the cameras, I was worried."

The inside of her house was sparse but beautiful. Fresh flowers in vases and tastefully chosen art pieces. It was comfortable too. Not something thrown together, it was *intentional*. I recognized it, because it was what I'd done with my own home. I'd made it mine, and she'd made hers truly her own.

Mara turned and went to the small kitchen across the space. A kettle steamed, and she pulled down a second mug for me. And suddenly tea was the furthest thing from my fucking mind because Mara was *limping*. "Are you okay?" I asked around a lump in my throat. "You're hurt?"

A tea bag in one mug, then one in the other. Her shoulders curved like she was ashamed of the fact that she was hurt.

"Mara." I cleared my throat. "Why do you need security cameras? Is there something we need to know? If there is, you know we'll protect you. You don't have to be alone, I promise."

She brought the mugs over to the coffee table and set them down, gently touching the bowl of sugar and the little creamer pitcher she'd set out for herself, offering them to me. Still, she didn't say anything out loud.

I wasn't sure if it was simply her normal silence or if she'd been triggered again, but her silence was devastating. It filled up the room, and I couldn't breathe around it. Mara needed help, and no matter if it was the most painful thing I'd ever do, I would get her help. Even if it wasn't from me.

"Mara, I don't know what's going on." I tried to keep my voice low and even. "But I can see something is wrong. I can *feel* it. If you don't want to talk to me, I'll go. Just tell me who I can bring for you to speak to. Is there anyone else you want me to call?"

She sat on the couch, staring into the middle distance, and I closed my eyes. A piece of my heart was shattering, and I hadn't even known it was at risk. One breath of her at the wedding, and my subconscious had claimed more than it had any right to.

"I'll check on you," I said quietly. "You can call me any time. I'll see if Evie can stop by later."

My hand was on her doorknob, and I heard her voice. "Liam."

When I looked back, her blue eyes were fixed on mine. She was scared. Fear lived in every line of her body. But she looked more scared that I would leave. "Wait."

Mara

LIAM WAS IN MY HOUSE.

I couldn't wrap my head around it. Liam was in my house, and I loved it as much as it terrified me, because I'd imagined a hundred different ways of him coming here for the first time, and none of them was this.

My voice still preferred to hide, but I could find it for him. Telling Liam the truth didn't scare me like it did when I thought about other people. Because he'd already seen me panic and helped me through it. I knew—or I hoped—he wouldn't judge me for it. Especially since I'd already let him in.

But that didn't mean it was easy.

His hand rested on the doorknob, ready to turn it, and all I wanted was for him *not* to go.

Thankfully, the relief was clear on his face. He didn't want to go either. Liam was the first one to come and see if I was okay.

Slowly, he came back and sat on the couch. Close enough to reach out and touch, far enough he wasn't crowding me. "What happened to your ankle?"

"I fell," I said quietly. "While—while I was setting up the cameras."

Now that I'd broken the silence, it felt easier. It was always easier once I started, but sometimes the silence was so loud and so impenetrable it felt impossible. "I'm okay," I told him. "It's already better. In a couple of days, I'll be good as new."

Exhaustion pulled me down. I was tired. I didn't want to be afraid. I wanted to take more control of my own life. I didn't want to be defined by this. But the reality was that once I told him, I could never go back.

I rubbed my palms on my knees to ease the nerves.

Liam leaned forward, elbows on his own knees. "Why do you need them? The cameras."

Pressing my lips together, I closed my eyes. "I grew up in a cult."

The air around me felt charged, and I opened my eyes to see the horror and disgust on Liam's face. But there wasn't

any to find. He was just looking at me, waiting for me to tell him more.

I could have gotten lost in staring at him. Because Liam looking at me like that? It was a dream come true.

"I mean, not at first. I wasn't born there. We joined when I was six, and we didn't know. It was supposed to be this great, communal place. My dad was gone, and for my mom, the idea of having help to raise us was too good to be true. And it was."

Blowing out a breath, I put a hand on my chest. So many words at once wasn't my normal, but this story had been waiting to come out of me for a long time.

I couldn't tell him everything yet—I wasn't ready for that, and he wasn't either. But I could tell him enough.

"But it wasn't that. It was…very different. My mom disappeared when I was thirteen. We'd been planning to leave, and then she just walked out our door one morning and never came back."

"Mara—"

I held out a hand. This story was one I needed to get through all in one go. "The leader, Malcolm Novic, he had his own beliefs and mandates. Including taking what he wanted from everyone. Including…" I shook my head. "He would choose girls and prepare them. Then they would be married to him. But through him, they would be married to every man in the commune. Shared.

"I was one of those girls."

Liam's eyes went wide, and I gathered all the courage I had left. "The compound was raided before it happened, when I was fifteen. I was young enough I hadn't known they were being investigated for exactly that—grooming and sex crimes. And I…I helped put him in jail."

He scrubbed a hand over his face and looked at me. There *was* horror there, but *for* me, not because of me.

My voice was quieter now, my steam running out. "The other day when you saw me, I'd gotten a package. Daniel opened it."

I couldn't keep my eyes off the box that sat on a table across the room. I hadn't moved it since I'd brought it back that day.

"May I?" he asked.

I nodded.

He stood and walked to the box, and in spite of myself, I watched the way he moved. He was graceful, the way all the Resting Warrior men were. But this was Liam. I couldn't keep my eyes off him.

He held the veil in his hands, and he was staring at it the same way I had—like it was coated in acid.

"He's still in jail," I whispered. "I don't know who sent it, and everything is…probably fine. But the cameras make me feel better."

"I'll help you put them up more securely," he said, the corner of his mouth turning up into a smile. "I don't think them falling down will make you feel better."

"Thank you."

Liam put the veil back into the box and carefully closed it. "I don't know what to say, Mara."

"It's a lot. I understand."

He truly smiled then. "But the one good thing is it's the most I've ever heard you talk."

My whole face flushed, and I stood, unable to keep still even though my ankle ached. "I—" I swallowed. "It's just that I already knew what to say, and—"

"Mara." Liam stepped toward me with his hands out. "It's not a bad thing. I love the sound of your voice. And, subject matter aside, I could listen to you talk forever."

His words froze me in my tracks.

He liked my voice?

To me, it always sounded too brassy and loud. It was an intrusion and not a welcome one. But when Liam said that, it made me question all of it. How many of those feelings about my voice were things I had learned because I'd been forced to cling to silence?

It was like the world shifted, and no one felt it but me.

Silence stretched between us once more, as my mind tried to make sense of everything happening. Liam liked my *voice*. For anyone else, that might sound like nothing, but all I'd ever known was to be wanted for my silence.

What did I do?

The question forced me to sit down again.

I wanted this, and I wanted him…whatever that meant for the two of us. But it wasn't something I fully understood or knew how to initiate. It felt like I was a million miles out at sea and Liam was the only land in sight.

And still, even after him telling me something so lovely, I was frozen. Like a block of ice or my flowers on a winter morning. Brittle and unable to move without breaking.

Liam's face, which had hosted a beautiful smile, fell. I didn't like the pain I saw in his eyes as he took in all of me. *All of me*. He took a step back, reversing all the distance he'd closed between us.

"I'm sorry," he said, clearing his throat. "That probably —that wasn't appropriate. I'm sorry, Mara. Forgive me for overstepping. Especially in your house."

No.

Emotion tumbled through my stomach. Liam hadn't done anything wrong, or anything I didn't want. But I didn't know how to tell him. All my words were evaporating like mist in the morning sun. How did people do this? How did anyone manage to say what they needed to say without drowning?

The rest had been easy because it was just a memory. I

didn't need to think about it; I just needed to recount it. This was so much fucking harder, and this was the moment where it truly mattered.

I couldn't let him think I didn't want this, because something deep in my gut told me if he left now, nothing would ever be the same between us again.

Liam's shoulders fell, and he turned toward the door. I stood so quickly I nearly fell over trying to balance on my ankle, and Liam turned, moving faster than I thought possible, catching me and keeping me steady.

His arm was around my waist, and I was remembering back to those moments at the wedding when he'd held me and everything felt safe and perfect. The way his arm fit around me felt like it was meant to be there.

"Mara?" Liam asked quietly. "Are you all right?"

I looked up at him, and I turned my body fully toward him. Intentionally, I curled my fingers into his shirt. "Please," I finally whispered.

He was so close, eyes filled with genuine concern—and so much more I wasn't sure I knew how to read. "Please what?"

My heart pounded in my ears. This was terrifying. Maybe the scariest thing I'd ever done in my life, though it was a different kind of fear. The kind of fear that could lead to *everything*.

I lifted my eyes to his. "Please don't go."

Chapter 7

Liam

"PLEASE DON'T GO."

Mara looked up at me, and she wasn't terrified. Not in the way I'd seen her at the wedding or at the hardware store —not in the way that shook me to my core.

What I saw in her eyes now was so much more than fear. It was fear, but also vulnerability. With relief, I realized she hadn't wanted me to walk away any more than I wanted to.

Her cheeks flushed and her breath came in tiny sips, almost like she was tasting the air. The way she was pressed against me, she was trembling. Asking me to stay had taken everything.

Another moment of clarity came on the heels of the first.

She'd spoken so easily about what had happened to her. As if she were a different person. But those were memories set in stone. Now she struggled to find the words she needed. That was fine. Though I loved the sound of her voice, Mara and I could live in silence if it meant I could be near her.

Slowly, I turned too, loving the feeling of her hands gripping my shirt and trying not to let those thoughts derail me. It would be so easy to let my mind fall into the fantasies I'd tried—and sometimes failed—to resist.

Mara still looked at me, worry starting to take over her beautiful face. I wouldn't let that happen. All I'd asked the universe for was a chance. Now that I had one, I would take it.

"You've done a lot of talking today," I said.

She breathed out a shaky sigh and nodded.

"Is it all right if I do a little more? All you have to do is listen."

Another nod, and her fingers tightened in my shirt. I wrapped my other arm around her in order to hold her more fully. I probably should have let her sit, but the idea of our being separated right now was unbearable.

"I remember the first time I saw you," I said. "You were working on the flower beds around the Ravali cabin right after it was built. I was walking from the stables, and there you were. You had your hair in a crown like you wore at the wedding, but it was windy enough that it was flying away from you. You were up to your elbows in dirt, but you were smiling so brightly I could see it from all the way across the field. And I thought you were the most beautiful woman I'd ever seen."

Her eyes widened, and I tried not to smile too broadly. How Mara could think she was anything less than stunning was a mystery, and yet now that I knew her story, it also made sense. But given the opportunity, not a day would go by that I didn't tell her.

"I loved seeing you whenever I could, and I'll never forget the first time you smiled at *me*. Some silly joke I made at family dinner, and you looked over and smiled right at me, and I think my heart stopped beating for a minute."

Mara's eyes were suddenly glassy, but I didn't stop speaking.

"The first time I heard your voice, it was a laugh. Just a soft one, from a distance. It was so unexpected, it stopped me in my tracks, and I don't think I ever really started walking again.

"I don't remember when I started looking for you around the ranch. It wasn't something I did on purpose, but at some point, I realized I was only happy at the end of the day when I'd seen you. I loved making you smile and laugh when I could, sharing little things with you. I liked getting to know you in the way you were comfortable."

I slid one hand up her spine until it curved around the back of her neck, recreating the breathless moment we'd shared outside the reception tent. "And then one day, I realized it wasn't just friendship I wanted. It was so much more than that. And I knew, too, it was something I would never force or move too fast, because this is your home. I never want to be the reason you feel uncomfortable, or worse, like you need to leave. Because you feel safe here, and your safety is more important than anything, Mara. It's more important than whatever I feel. I need you to know that."

She nodded quickly, lips pressed together. She knew.

My heart ached in my chest, either because it was so full or because I was finally releasing everything I'd felt for her.

"I'm not perfect," I said quietly, gut tightening. "And I don't know if I deserve someone like you. I never want to hurt you. But I also want to help you with whatever you need, Mara. I don't care if it's installing security cameras, protecting you from a truck belt breaking, or facing your past. It doesn't matter. I want to help you."

Mara's breath was as shallow as mine, and her gaze dropped to my lips before returning. I could see desire there. It threatened to put me on my knees.

"All of that to say, this isn't a whim for me. It's not a fling. I want you. I want all of you, and if that's something you want too, I want to try this." I took a breath. "And if you'll let me, I very much want to kiss you."

No sound penetrated the silence around the two of us. Mara was so still she'd stopped breathing, staring at me. Her knuckles were white, squeezing my shirt, but she wasn't pushing me away.

She was pulling me closer.

"Yes."

The softest, smallest word in the world.

And it changed everything.

I leaned in, pressing my lips to hers. The number of times I'd imagined this moment…

This was so much better.

Mara made a soft noise, which made me go blind with the need to yank her against my body and kiss her harder. To consume her the way she'd consumed my mind all this time.

But I held back, keeping the kiss between us soft and slow. She tasted like the tea she'd made for us and a sweeter flavor that reminded me of her floral scent. God, this woman undid me.

Dizziness wrapped around me like I was falling and she was the only thing keeping me grounded.

Drawing back, I pulled her close and kissed her forehead, wrapping her up tightly, one hand in her hair and the other low on her hip. She was so small, yet I felt the strength in her. Anyone who had gone through what she had was made of steel.

And still, I wanted to protect her however I could.

It wasn't lost on me how Mara was holding me back just as tightly as I held her. Just like we had at Grant and Cori's wedding, but so much more than that.

Many times in my life, I'd wondered if I'd ever hold someone like this again. And with Mara?

Nothing had ever felt more right.

Who knew how long it took the two of us to pull away from each other. Neither of us was in a hurry. No people waited to see where we'd gone, and no one would judge us for the indulgence.

But slowly, we leaned apart so we could see each other, and Mara was relaxed. She smiled at me, no more fear or worry in her eyes. They were calm and happy, like I always wanted them to be.

Still, I nearly held my breath when I asked her, "Will you try this with me?"

She nodded, tucking her face briefly into my shirt. But not before I saw the blush on her cheeks. I would keep it there permanently if I could. "Will you go on a date with me?"

A silly grin crossed her face when she pulled back to look at me, eyes sparkling with *yes* even before she nodded.

I couldn't stop the smile on my face either. "I have one more question."

She raised her eyebrows, and I smiled again. It didn't matter if Mara wasn't talking. She was still one of the most expressive people I'd ever met.

"At the wedding, I'm not sure if you noticed, but people were watching us."

"Yeah," she whispered quietly.

"Jude knows that I've liked you, and the rest of them are all over me to make sure I'm good to you. Even though it was only one dance."

Mara laughed softly. It wasn't completely unexpected. The Resting Warrior family protected their own, and she had to know she was a part of it.

"But I want to know how open you want to be about it. I

won't be offended if you don't want to tell anyone yet. Seems like you have a lot going on." I glanced over at the box with the bridal veil inside it.

Something I needed to process later. It wasn't like I didn't know men like the ones she described existed. My awareness was even greater because of everything that had happened since we'd moved here and opened the ranch. But hearing this beautiful woman talk about being groomed to be a toy for an entire population of men wasn't easy. While she was a *child*.

Reaching up, I tucked a stray piece of hair behind her ear, and I savored the way she closed her eyes, leaning into the touch. If there was one single thing I would do in my life, it would be to make sure I was always worthy of the kind of trust that tiny movement showed.

When she opened her eyes, I saw her hesitation. And I knew it had nothing to do with me. This wasn't going to be easy for her, to begin with. Doing it with an audience would only make it harder.

Mara swallowed. "Not yet."

Leaning down, I touched my forehead to hers. "Okay."

"Not forever." Her whisper was so quiet I nearly missed it.

"I know." I cut myself off before I could call her *sweet-heart*. It felt like the most natural thing in the world, and yet I didn't want to push her too fast. I was ready to dive into the ocean that was Mara with my entire being, but she needed to set the pace. I would do the rest.

"I'll plan something for us," I said. "Just the two of us. And if you have anything you want, please tell me. And I don't just mean about the date. Anything."

She tightened her hands on my arms.

"If you're scared, you can call me. You don't even have

to speak. If you need help with something, I can be here in no time at all, and I want to be."

Tilting her face up to mine, I kissed her again. I couldn't stop myself. The taste of her lips was too sweet, and now that I'd had one chance to feel them under mine, I knew I would never get enough.

I slowly pulled away, wishing I didn't have to let her go. But the same instincts that had called me to her house were now telling me I needed to give her space.

"I'll see you soon?" I asked.

Mara bit her lip and nodded.

It was torture to make myself turn and leave her house, but I did, looking back one more time to find her watching me. I smiled and left, knowing that if I didn't, I wouldn't be able to make myself say goodbye.

Chapter 8

Mara

THE PHONE RANG on speaker in Rayne's office, and I twisted my hands together before letting them go once more. Stillness wasn't what I wanted right now. Nerves building under my skin made me want to move or do something with my hands. I forced them under my legs.

The flower beds on the ranch were a nicer place to be. Or even catching up on all the work I'd missed because of my ankle, rather than sitting here having to have this conversation. And yet, it needed to happen, so Rayne was making it happen.

"Claire Marshall." My lawyer's familiar voice answered the phone.

It took me a second to find my voice, and Rayne reached over to touch my shoulder.

"Hello?"

"It's Mara Greene," I said.

"Oh." She sounded surprised. "Hello, Mara. You're on

my list of people to call this week, so this is a nice coincidence."

"Ms. Marshall, this is Dr. Rayne Westerfield, Mara's therapist. We've spoken before."

"Of course. Hello, Dr. Westerfield."

Rayne encouraged me to do as much talking as I could on these calls, but I couldn't always, and it was nice to have someone who could take over when everything was too overwhelming.

"Unfortunately, the timing of this call isn't as coincidental as you think."

There was a brief silence. "Has something happened?"

I took a long, slow breath. "I received a package. There was no name attached to it, but the veil was inside it."

"*The* veil? The one from the commune?"

"Yes," I confirmed and looked at Rayne.

"Mara came to me when she received the package, obviously concerned about both the contents and the origin of it. We called the prison where Novic is being held to confirm he was still in custody and were informed about the parole hearing."

Claire sighed. "Yes, that was why I was going to call you. Because of good behavior over the length of his time served, he applied for parole and was granted a hearing. It's not guaranteed, but it would help a lot if you came down and testified."

Cold fear splashed down on me like a wave. I stood, pacing across Rayne's office. The last thing I wanted in the entire world was to see Malcolm Novic again. He starred in enough of my nightmares and flashbacks without having to see his face and update what he looked like—or worse, see he was still the same man who went to prison and nothing had changed.

"We'll come back to that in a minute," Rayne said. "Do you know if he sent the package to Mara?"

"No." Claire's response was immediate. "Malcolm doesn't have any personal effects in prison, and he doesn't have mail privileges. I'll double-check with the warden, but I can almost guarantee he didn't send it. However, if he ordered someone to send it, that's harder to pin down. And I doubt we'd be able to prove it."

She wasn't wrong. He could have visitors, and even though the cult had been disbanded, there were surely some who still visited him.

I shuddered. Malcolm was a charismatic man. Charming. There was a reason he was able to pull people in and make them believe what he wanted them to believe. It had taken me a long time to see the truth of it, but now I had. I also knew that the kind of influence he exerted on people's minds didn't just go away.

Even after I helped him get sent to prison, years had gone by before I'd fully understood I wasn't guilty or at fault for anything that had been done to me. Every time I took a beating for some perceived infraction or looking in the wrong direction. And then he was all smiles and love.

"Good, thank you," Rayne said. "Please confirm with Mara when you hear from the prison."

"I will. Mara." Claire's voice was now directed straight at me. "I know you probably don't want to come and testify, but I need you to."

Wrapping my arms around myself, I shook my head. "I don't know if I can."

"Of course you can. You did it the first time, and you've come so far since then."

"Claire—" I swallowed. "I don't want to see him."

She sighed, her disappointment palpable through the phone. "I know. And if you *really* think you can't handle it, you can send a witness impact statement. But I need to tell you that those aren't very effective. Compared to seeing a living, breathing person who's been affected by someone's crimes? Letters are easy to ignore. Especially with someone like Malcolm, who will be able to talk almost anyone over to his side."

All the heat had left my body, and I couldn't seem to get warm. Goose bumps covered my skin, and they weren't going away even as I rubbed my arms. "I don't know."

Rayne watched me carefully.

"Listen," Claire said. "There were a lot of things that contributed, but your testimony was a huge part of his conviction. Still, these were largely invisible crimes. To some people, especially those who weren't there at the original trial, they're going to look at this man and wonder if twelve years is long enough. Maybe he served his time, and maybe it wasn't all that bad."

Rayne opened her mouth to say something, but Claire kept going, not giving her a chance to speak at all. "If you don't come and do this, the chances are high he'll be released. And then what? He'll be free to find other girls and groom them the same way he did you. He did it once, and he'll do it again. Is that what you want, Mara?"

"No."

"I didn't think so."

Now Rayne looked angry. "This is a difficult enough decision for Mara without you using her emotions and guilt against her, Claire."

"I'm just telling her the truth. If she wants to protect other people, she needs to do this."

Rayne's mouth formed a thin line, and I didn't know what to say. She wasn't wrong, and yet the idea of saying yes right this second made me want to run to the bathroom and be sick.

Leaning down, Rayne muted the phone. "Could you decide by tomorrow?"

I chewed on my lip. "I think so."

Unmuting, she picked up the handset. "We're going to discuss it, and Mara will give you a yes or no answer tomorrow. And whatever the answer is, my expectation is that you'll respect it."

Another sigh filtered through the phone. "Of course."

"Good. You'll hear from her soon."

She ended the call and leaned farther back in her chair, watching me where I still stood.

Rayne never pressured me to be any one way. If I needed to stand and walk around, then that's what I did. Right now, I needed to be on my feet. It felt safer. Like I could run if I wanted to, even though there was nothing to run from here.

"I don't like the way she's pressuring you," Rayne said.

I shook my head. Obviously, I didn't like it either. "But she's not wrong."

Spreading her hands open, Rayne shrugged. "Will there be a benefit to your testimony? I'm sure there would be. But whether Malcolm Novic receives parole does *not* rest on your shoulders, Mara. The committee that's in charge of the hearing has a duty to look at all the evidence of his crimes committed, along with the new testimony during this hearing.

"Even if you do testify, the decision lies with them. And of course, you could testify, and he could still be released. I just want to make sure you know that this is not your responsibility."

Of course, she was right. My stomach still churned with nerves and anxiety because of what Claire had said. If he got out and did to more girls what he'd done to others and tried to do to me, it wouldn't be *entirely* my fault. But I would have had a hand in it, and I wasn't sure I could live with myself.

"I need to think about it."

She nodded. "Whatever you decide, make sure it's right for you. And however you choose, we'll deal with it."

"Thank you."

It was the end of our time, our having talked about things before the call. I said goodbye to Rayne, glad to know she supported the idea of Liam and me. When I told him I didn't want to tell anyone, I didn't count Rayne because she wasn't allowed to tell anyone. Next time I saw him, I would let him know.

I wasn't quite ready to go home yet. Everything Claire said was circling around in my head, and I still needed the sensation of movement. The ranch truck was parked outside Rayne's office, but Deja Brew wasn't far. I would walk down and grab a drink before heading home.

Lena and Evie never gave me a hard time if I wasn't up to talking, and Lena always knew what I needed without fail. It was her superpower, and everyone knew it.

The door to the coffee shop opened quickly, and I had to pull up short. A woman came out, nearly running into me, and she pulled up short too.

"Oh!" She put a hand on her chest. "It's you. I really need to stop doing that. Seems like every time I see you, I'm nearly knocking you over. At least you weren't holding anything this time."

It took me a second to place her.

She held out a hand. I shook it automatically. "I'm Brynn, by the way."

Brynn. Oh. She was the woman I'd run into leaving Rayne's office the other day after the veil arrived. Rayne had said her name. "Mara," I managed to say quietly.

"Mara." Brynn lit up. "I'm so sorry I ran into you the

other day. I just moved here, and I'm a total mess. But I'm trying to get to know people."

She stepped around me. "Listen, I'd stay and try to chat for a minute, but I'm actually on my way to see Rayne. But I hope I'll see you around!"

Before I could even think about whether I could speak, she was gone down the sidewalk in the direction I'd just come from. She seemed nice, from the thirty seconds we'd been in each other's company.

Anyone who was seeing Rayne got immediate points in my book. As a therapist, she worked with many kinds of clients. But she didn't work with people like Malcolm. There were no prisons nearby, and all the bad apples Resting Warrior had encountered were now far from here.

But Brynn seemed like someone people would like. I wouldn't say I was the authority on instinctually judging someone's character, but I was getting better.

I went inside, and Lena immediately saw me and smiled. "Hey, Mara. It's been a while since I saw you in here."

Nodding, I smiled back. It had been a while since I'd been in town. After the call, my words were gone. Instead, I placed my hand over my heart.

Evie stuck her head out of the kitchen and waved.

"You want your regular?"

I gave Lena a thumbs-up, and I went to the comfy chairs that were placed off to the side. What was I going to do? Flying down to Arizona to see my worst nightmare wasn't on my list of priorities.

My phone buzzed in my pocket, and I pulled it out. Liam's name on the screen made me smile.

Are you free tomorrow?

I answered immediately.

73

Yes.

Tomorrow was Saturday. My work hours weren't set in stone, and I often did work on weekends, but no one would mind if I didn't. And I wanted to see him. My stomach did little flip-flops just thinking about it. I wanted him to kiss me again.

I'll meet you around 1? At your house. We've got a drive ahead of us.

Where are we going?

The little bubbles popped up and faded away.

How do you feel about surprises?

In general I wasn't a fan. Mostly because the surprises in my life up until now hadn't been good ones. But this was Liam. I couldn't imagine any surprise he could come up with would be bad.

I don't mind if they're from you.

Then I'll keep it a surprise. 😉

That added winking smile had butterflies starting in my chest.

"What has you smiling like that?" Lena asked as she put the cold cup down in front of me. It had a domed lid on the top that was absolutely packed with whipped cream.

"Nothing," I whispered.

Evie sat down on my other side and nudged me with her shoulder. "You sure? Because your smile is exactly the kind of smile Lena used to get whenever Jude came in to visit. And we all know how that ended."

I blushed but said nothing, reaching for the drink and the straw and busying myself with unwrapping it and sliding it inside.

"We're teasing, Mara. It's good to see you smiling. And I'm sure whatever—or whoever—is the source is well worth it."

They were definitely right about that, and I was now eager to see what Liam had planned for us tomorrow. I looked over at Evie. "Where's Avery?"

She sighed. "Lucas is on dad duty. I needed to get out of the house."

Lena snorted. "You could have gone anywhere, Evie. You didn't have to come in and work."

"Where else would I go?" She shrugged. "It feels good to do something like normal. Avery is everything we ever dreamed, but it feels good to be the old Evie too."

I smiled at her. Evie and Lucas's daughter was beautiful, and I was more than a little jealous. One of the things I actually missed about being at the compound was all the children. They hadn't been connected to any of the bad things; they simply *were*. Kids were joyous and uncomplicated. They just wanted what they wanted, and that was the end of it.

Someday, with the right person, I wanted them.

A different set of nerves tumbled in my gut. Was Liam that person? Way, *way* too soon to be thinking anything of the sort. And yet, my mind was now filled with images of Liam running around with a kid who looked like both of us, and my heart grew in my chest.

"See?" Lena said. "She's not even here."

My friend winked at me, and I realized they'd been talking while I was daydreaming about Liam and babies. "Sorry."

"Nothing to be sorry for," Lena said. A chime over the door drew our attention as a new customer came in. Leaning in, Lena put her hand on my shoulder. "It was really good to see you, Mara. I hope you come in more often, and when you're ready to tell us why you're smiling, we're all ears."

They left me alone to help the customer, and I grabbed my drink, heading back to my truck. Just that small interaction and the short walk made me feel much calmer.

This was my life now. I had good friends, a good support system, and if things went well, a good relationship. In spite of my problems with speaking, I wasn't the girl who'd arrived at Resting Warrior, the one still running from her problems and still not making any progress.

No matter what, I had these things. They weren't going away because of a shadow from my past. Was it still scary? Yes. Was I sure I could handle it? No.

But I needed to try.

As soon as I got back to my house, I opened my email and told Claire I would testify.

Chapter 9

Liam

AT ONE O'CLOCK SHARP, I pulled up to Mara's house in my truck. I'd been ready for hours, and waiting to see her felt like torture, but I'd made myself wait until the time we agreed on. We were spending the whole day together—there would be plenty of time.

Now that we were giving this a shot, I needed to fight against wanting to make up for everything we'd missed. There was no missing anything. Everything was still in front of us.

I lifted my hand to knock on the door, and it opened before I could. Mara was standing there, and I was stunned into silence. She wasn't smiling, her face nervous, but she was absolutely fucking breathtaking.

After all this time, I knew Mara well enough to know when she was relaxed and when she wasn't. There was tension in her body, but when I reached out for her, she didn't pull away.

Waiting until she gave me the okay, I kissed her. The tension in her body melted away, and it was going to be a long day. Because her reaction had *my* body reacting, and as much as I wanted every part of her, I would wait an eternity until Mara was ready.

When I pulled back, Mara was smiling. It was enough to tell me I wasn't the reason she was nervous. "Hi," I said.

"Hi." Her voice was soft but clear. I took her hand, and she shut and locked the door behind her.

I helped her up into the truck and closed the door before going around to the driver's side. Reaching across the seat, she put her hand in mine immediately. Her small smile told me she was excited. Even if she was a little nervous.

"Are you going to tell me?"

"Do you want to know?"

As she pressed her lips together, I recognized the motion as one of her thinking. Then she blew out a breath. "I trust you."

"Thank you."

Pulling out of the ranch, I aimed away from town. It was a far drive, but it would be worth it.

For a while, we rode in silence, just hand in hand. But there was nothing awkward about the quiet. It was just as peaceful as the moments we'd shared when we ran into each other on the ranch.

But I could give her a hint about where we were going. "Working at Resting Warrior, have you learned much about how Navy SEALs train?"

Mara looked over at me and shook her head.

That made sense. It wasn't our focus on the ranch and not something we always talked about. "Well, I'm not going to bore you about all of it, I promise. But if you could guess, what would you say was my favorite part?"

After a moment, her fingers fluttered in my hold. "I don't know," she said quietly. "Something with water?"

I smiled, loving the sound of her voice. "A lot of people guess that. Especially because it was the Navy. Don't get me wrong, I'm a good swimmer. But it was actually the air training I loved. By all rights, I probably should have gone into the Air Force, but I wanted to be a SEAL."

"Why?"

Shrugging, I squeezed her hand. "They're the best of the best. I wanted to be the best at something."

Her curiosity was plain, and a time would come when I would tell her all about my past and *why* I'd always wanted to be the best. But that was a bit heavy for a first date. As it was, taking Mara two hours away from home was already pushing the first-date protocol.

"But it was the air. As soon as they told us we'd be para- chuting, it was like everything made sense. The first time I jumped out of a plane, my whole mind went quiet. Every- thing felt *free* and right. I can't really explain it except to say I fell in love with flying, and I miss it every day. Some of my teammates used to joke that I must have been a bird in another life."

Mara smiled. I saw when I glanced over. "What kind of bird?"

I chuckled. "Not sure. Depends on who you ask. If it were any of my team, they might say a bird of prey. Falling from the sky and dealing death from above. But I'm not sure my life now resembles that. Maybe a mockingbird. Or a crow. A bird with a sense of humor."

The road passed us for a while before I spoke again. "What kind of animal would you be?"

She thought again, her mouth twisting up. Then she spoke. All this time, her voice had been quiet, and it still was.

But there was an ease to it now. "I don't know what other people would say. But I would like to be a cat."

"Stealthy and fierce?"

She nodded.

Eventually, the signs for Missoula came into view, and it was time to give her a little more information about what we were doing. "Have you ever wanted to do anything like I described? Jumping out of an airplane with a parachute?"

"I—" She blinked. "I don't know."

I squeezed her hand. "I promise we're not jumping out of anything. But we'll be in the air."

I caught her looking at me out of the corner of my eye since I was still driving.

"Missoula is one of the oldest paragliding spots in the United States," I told her. "The mountains are made for it. I thought it would be good for the both of us," I clarified. "There's no reason you need to speak, and I'll get a taste of the air again."

We didn't need to go all the way into the city to get where we were going. That could come after.

"We're flying?" she asked.

"If it's okay with you." I held my breath. It was a risk to plan something like this on a first date, and I'd sketched out a few alternatives in case we got here and Mara was terrified or didn't trust me enough to fly with me. But I hoped she would.

Her voice was a whisper of a whisper. "Can I go with you?"

As in, she didn't want to be alone. "It was the only way we'd do it," I promised.

"Okay."

I turned the truck off the road and made my way to the paragliding facility where they'd give us a rundown of the procedures and equipment before taking us up the mountain. And the whole time, I watched Mara, staying within touching distance. She said nothing, but she watched everything.

Her eyes were bright with curiosity, not fear. When we got into the truck to go up the mountain with our instructor, she tucked herself into me. I put an arm around her waist and pulled her closer, kissing her temple and enjoying the scent of her hair.

I never used to understand when people said they did that, but now I was obsessed. There was nothing quite like it. "Are you nervous?" I whispered in her ear.

She nodded, and I tightened my arm around her waist. "I've got you, Mara."

I didn't just mean with what we were about to do. I meant everything. What I had said the other day, I meant. Whatever she needed, whenever she needed it, I wanted to be there.

The prep was quick once we got to the top of the mountain, the wind blowing us every which way. Mara got strapped to my chest, and I couldn't resist the urge to brush a kiss to the back of her head. "Ready?"

Her nod was shaky, but it was there. She was going to love this.

The wing spread out behind us, caught by the wind and rising above us. We ran toward the edge, and already, I felt the lift created by the fabric overhead. There was always going to be something terrifying about running straight toward open air, but our feet weren't even touching the ground by the time we reached it.

We swooped into open space together, Mara gasping as we dropped and *flew*.

The valley was laid out in front of us, city sparkling in the afternoon sun. The wind was clear and cold, and my mind embraced the blissful quiet that only came from being airborne.

It had been too long since I'd done this, and there was no one I'd rather share it with than Mara.

Slowly, she released her grip on the harness and held out her hands, feeling the air between her fingers as we soared through the sky. My only regret at this moment was that I couldn't see her face.

"Are you all right?"

She nodded so quickly that I laughed, banking us toward where we needed to go.

There was something about adrenaline and hanging in open space. It created bonds nothing else could cause, like any experience that was unique. This would always be ours, Mara's and mine.

She laughed as we descended, and I wished I could give her more. Freeze time and gravity to make it last forever. But our feet had to touch the ground sometime. As soon as we did and our harnesses were unstrapped, I pulled her to me. Mara's face was flushed from the wind, eyes sparkling with pure joy. I couldn't remember a time I'd seen her look more alive.

I kissed her.

Not like before. Not careful and hesitant to make sure we didn't go too fast. I kissed her the way I *craved* to kiss her, hard and deep, putting everything I'd ever imagined into it.

Mara kissed me back.

She wound her arms around my neck, and we fell into each other. One of the instructors laughed, and we broke apart, but nothing could stop the smiles on either of our faces.

"Thank you," she said quietly.

"It was my pleasure. You really liked it?"

With her arms still around my neck, she was pressed

against me in every possible way, and I was doing my best not to be distracted. "It felt like freedom."

"*Yes*. Exactly."

The drive back to my truck was quick, and I drove over to the next destination in my plan—a meal in one of Missoula's many parks before we made the long journey back home.

"Is that something you'd like to do again?" I asked.

"Yes." Mara's voice was quiet again. "Sometime. Later."

Something about the word later made my instincts sit up and listen. The food I'd brought in a cooler was simple but good. I laid it out, and Mara pulled her knees up to her chest, closing herself off. Something had distracted her and taken her away from me. I didn't think she'd been triggered, but it wasn't always easy to know.

"Mara?" I asked, reaching out and picking up her hand.

She looked at me, smiling. But the smile was empty compared to what it had been.

"Where did you go?"

"Sorry," she whispered.

I shook my head. "That's not what I meant. Are you okay?"

"Yes and no." She shook her head. "Here? Now? This is amazing. I was just thinking…"

I waited, handing her a sandwich and a drink and watching her begin to eat.

"What I told you the other day. The man I put in jail is having a parole hearing. Last night, I said I'd testify, and I was so sure. But thinking about it has me in knots. When I said later—I can't think about anything past that."

Understandable.

"When is it?"

"Next week."

My eyebrows rose. That was soon. "You're going alone?"

She shrugged and looked away.

"You don't have to."

When she looked back at me, her beautiful eyes were filled with that same vulnerability.

"Whatever you need, Mara. If you need me to support you from afar, I will. If you want me beside you every step of the way? I'll do that too. Whatever you need."

"Really?"

"Really. But I recommend talking to Daniel and Jude. If there's anything to know that the court isn't telling you, they'll be the ones able to find it."

Mara went pale. "What would there be to find?"

"I don't know. But if there was something, it's better to know before you get there."

"You're right."

Putting my food aside, I moved closer to her. "Thank you for telling me."

She was the one to reach out this time, pulling on the fabric of my shirt until I was close enough. And she kissed me. My eyes stayed open in surprise for a long moment before I let myself go. The food was forgotten entirely. We could eat any time. I would kiss Mara as long as she was willing to kiss me.

The way she pulled me closer, I lost my balance, taking us down onto the grass. She was underneath me, and *god*, it was everything. We weren't ready for that. I knew it, and still, I was disappointed that we were outside in the middle of a park and not somewhere closer to home and privacy.

"Liam?" Mara asked, breaking away far enough to see my face.

"Mara." I said her name because it was music. She deserved to hear it said.

Her whole face and neck were flushed, and it wasn't from the cold of the wind. She was looking at my mouth instead of at me. "Will you…" She took a deep breath. "Will you come with me?"

"To the hearing?"

She nodded, still not meeting my eyes.

Slowly, I lifted a hand and eased it behind her neck so I could guide her gaze to mine. There was the true fear. Deeper than the hearing itself. She was afraid I would tell her no, and that she would be abandoned and alone. Like she had been when her mother disappeared or when she'd suddenly lost everything she'd ever known, despite her world being twisted.

"Of course I will," I said quietly. "Of course."

She dug her fingers into my arms. "I'm scared."

"That's okay," I said. "It's okay to be scared. I'll be with you every step of the way. You're not alone in this."

She closed her eyes, and I kissed her again. When we finally separated, she was smiling again, and her expression was easy with relief. Mara's voice was almost unnecessary. She told me so much without words.

In that moment, she might feel like she was the one who needed me. But as we walked back to the truck hand in hand, I knew I was the one who needed her.

More than anything.

Chapter 10

Mara

I TOOK Liam's advice and slowly, painfully, told Daniel and Jude the truth. Not all of it, but enough to let them know what I needed and why I needed it.

Daniel was relieved to know the truth about the veil. Or at least a piece of it.

My fear of being treated differently was completely unfounded. Their only concern had been for me and how they could help. I felt foolish for worrying.

But going to the lodge on Monday morning because they'd asked to see me had my stomach in knots. I'd been alternating back and forth between joy and happiness because of Liam and our date, along with a dose of dread about the upcoming hearing and what could happen.

What if Malcolm really had found a way to send me the veil? Right before he had the possibility of getting out? It was terrifying, and there was no way to deny it was a threat. Even if it *wasn't* Malcolm, at best, it was someone trying to scare me. At worst…

I didn't want to think about the worst.

Jude and Daniel were in the security office, and both of them looked relaxed and happy. Not like they were about to deliver news that would devastate me. That was good.

"Hey, Mara," Daniel called. "You want some coffee?"

I shook my head. I had too much anxiety in my stomach to put anything in it. Later. I could have coffee later once I knew what they'd found.

"Come on in," Daniel said, gesturing to one of the chairs by the table. I sat and looked between them.

Jude lifted a small file folder in his hand. "This is everything we managed to find on Malcolm and The Family since the time of his arrest."

He put the folder in front of me, and I was relieved it was so thin. I opened it, and the first thing was a map. I recognized the layout, even though it was from above. The compound.

"The Family still exists, as far as we know the compound still exists, and the property is in Malcolm Novic's name. But after looking at the property via satellite, it doesn't seem to be an *active* site. Only a couple people came and went, and nothing to make me think anyone is living there."

I nodded. It made sense. After Malcolm was arrested and convicted, no one wanted to be swept up in the same wave. Especially not knowing what Malcolm would say to the authorities. Most of them ran. If I were them, I wouldn't go back to the same place either.

Daniel turned to face me more fully. "We reached out to whoever we could to learn anything about Malcolm in prison, and nothing came up. It might be on the side of a little *too* squeaky-clean, but there's no proof of tampering that we can see."

Slowly, I took a breath. "What does that mean?"

"It means one of two things," Daniel said. "Either someone is covering up whatever he's doing on the inside and making his record appear spotless."

"My money's on option number one," Jude said. "Simply because men like Malcolm Novic, in my experience, don't just become model citizens because they go to prison. But like we said, there's no proof, and it could just be me being overly suspicious."

Daniel chuckled. "But we like that about you."

The fact that he could laugh made me feel better. He wasn't one to make light of something if it were truly serious. "The other possibility," he said, "is Malcolm really *was* on his best behavior and kept himself squeaky-clean intentionally so he would have a chance like this one."

I turned over the map and skimmed the few pages they'd included with confirmations that nothing was amiss with Malcolm. Everything was going perfectly well, and he was a model prisoner.

"He'll get out?" My voice was barely a whisper, but it was all I had right now.

"There's no guarantee," Jude said. "There never is with hearings like this. But with a record like this, no incidents in the past…twelve years?" He winced. "There's a good chance he will. I'm sorry, Mara."

There was a good chance he would go free. But there was a better chance of him staying locked up if I testified.

All of a sudden, I felt dizzy.

I really had to do this.

The truth was right in front of my face. I'd agreed to testify, but I'd been hoping for a way out. A loophole we could use to make sure the hearing didn't even happen. Because it was close and it was *real* and I was going to have to see him again.

He would be in the same room with me. I would be able to look him in the eye, and at the same time, I didn't want to, knowing what he wanted to make me do.

"Come in, Mara."

I went into the office slowly. We weren't allowed in here. Not even to clean. The room was too big, and it was dusty because none of us were allowed inside. But it was pretty too. There were books. *I wondered if I would be allowed to come in and read them now since he was calling me.*

"Do you know why you're here today, Mara?"

"No."

"Well, come here, and I'll tell you." He gestured around the desk, and I didn't want to obey. The only time you went near Malcolm was to be punished, and I hadn't done anything to be punished. I had been so careful.

Swallowing, I made my way around the desk, closer to him. My hands were shaking, so I hid them behind my back.

"Are you scared, Mara?"

"N-no."

His face hardened. "You remember what you were told about lying? Are you scared of me?"

I swallowed again. "Yes."

"You don't have to be today." His smile was creepy. "Today, I have good news for you. I've told everyone to start making you a very special gown. It will take a while, but it is well worth the wait. Do you know what I mean?"

True fear built up in my chest. I knew, even if I didn't fully under-stand it yet. "I think so."

"It's you," he said. "I've chosen you to be the next bride of honor. When your gown and veil are ready, we will marry. You'll live with me and the other brides in the manor house. Would you like that?"

He reached out and stroked my cheek, and I didn't know how to respond. I wouldn't like it. But I also couldn't say no. You didn't say no to Malcolm. Ever. Everyone knew you said yes. And the last bride of honor still had bruises all over her whenever I saw her. And Adrian almost never spent the night in the manor house. She was always at other houses, doing things I wished I didn't know about but always heard in whispers.

So I forced a smile on my face and said, "Of course. Thank you."

"Good. I'll announce it this evening. Go back to your chores."

Leaving his office and closing the door behind me, I changed my mind. I never wanted to go into that room ever again.

"Mara?" Daniel's voice brought me back from the memory, but I still wasn't really here. I needed to get out. I needed to not be here. I needed to hide so I could be quiet and he wouldn't notice. If I was quiet enough, he wouldn't find me and he wouldn't make me marry him. I didn't want to marry him.

My breath came in gasps, and it felt like there wasn't enough air in the world to fill my lungs. Why couldn't I *breathe*?

"Mara." My name was gentle, but it sounded like him. Too slick and smooth and charming. I didn't want it. I didn't want him.

"Don't touch her." I heard a voice. "And don't get too close."

"Who do we call?"

"I think we both have a guess."

Why were they talking? Talking would give us away. They needed to be quiet. "Shh." I tried to be quiet. "He'll hear you."

There was no more talking after that. Only blissful silence. All I had to do was wait. Wait and everything would be fine. Wait until I knew he wasn't close, and I didn't have to see him or risk his attention.

"Mara?"

It was a different voice, and suddenly, my mind cleared. I was still in the security office in the chair I'd been sitting in before. Only, Daniel and Jude were no longer here, and Liam was crouching in front of me.

Oh no.

I looked around, chills running over my skin. "What did I do?"

"You didn't do anything," he said. "You just got caught up in your mind. You're okay."

I shook my head. It wasn't true. I wasn't okay. I wasn't fucking okay. I didn't want to go testify. I didn't want to see him.

"Are you okay if I touch you?"

One nod.

Coming up higher on his knees, he wrapped his arms around me, and I melted into his embrace. My breathing eased and my heart settled. In Liam's arms, the world was safe and *good*. I'd jumped off a mountain with this man, and he kept me alive.

I shuddered, embarrassment rushing up in the wake of reality. I'd just made a fool of myself in front of my bosses. It was them who'd been talking, and I *shushed* them.

"Let me take you home," Liam said quietly. "Will that make it better? Could you talk to me there?"

Every instinct I had told me not to talk. Silence was the only way to keep myself safe. But it wasn't the truth—it was years of habits. Talking was the true way to keep myself safe. But Liam was right. Home was better.

"Okay."

He helped me up, leading me out of the security office. Daniel was standing by the sink, and I froze, looking at the ground. It would only be so much worse later. "I'm sorry, Daniel."

When he turned around, he looked surprised. "There's nothing to apologize for. Absolutely nothing. If you need anything, please tell us. Whatever you need, we want to help."

I looked away, still embarrassed, even though I knew I shouldn't be. I filtered through the scents and sounds around me, pulling myself fully into my body. *Don't push it, Mara.* I heard Rayne's voice in my head.

She was right. I didn't need to push myself when I wasn't in a good space.

And there was no one who would say I was in a good space right now.

Liam helped me up into the truck I used and drove us back to my house. He hadn't been inside since that first time, having picked me up and dropped me off at the door for our date.

This time, I wanted him to come inside, though I wasn't sure what good it would do. I was broken. End of story. Soon enough, he was going to realize I wasn't worth it.

He followed me inside, waiting a step behind me while I unlocked the door. I shut it behind him and locked it. My breath immediately released. Here, I was safe. I had the cameras, the doors were locked, and Liam was with me.

"They called you?" I asked, going to the kitchen and pouring myself a glass of water.

"Jude did. Daniel suspected, like I said. I didn't tell them."

I drank all the water in one go. After things like this, you didn't realize how thirsty you were. "I wouldn't have minded if you had."

"Sure about that?" His voice was closer now. I kept leaning on the counter, and he touched my shoulder. When I didn't pull away, he stepped up and wrapped me in a hug.

"I'm sure," I whispered. "I'm just embarrassed they had to see that."

"You don't—"

"I know." I sighed, my throat nearly closing up to stop myself from speaking. "I know I don't need to be. But I'm still there."

Liam leaned his chin over my shoulder, the simple gesture reminding me how comfortable this was. I didn't want to use Liam as a crutch, but he made me feel so safe, it was hard not to crave it all the time. "Come sit with me," he said. "Tell me what happened."

On the couch, he tucked me into his side, and I enjoyed the casual way he could touch me and how I wasn't afraid of it. I did tell him what happened. Going to Arizona terrified me, and even though I'd said I would go, deep down, I'd been hoping for a way out. That clearly didn't happen.

"You can always email your lawyer and tell her you changed your mind," Liam said. "Nothing will happen to you if you decide not to go."

"You're right." I turned my face into his shoulder. "I know you're right. But the reasons I agreed in the first place are still true. If he gets out, and he tries again… If anyone gets hurt because I couldn't handle it, I wouldn't know how to live with myself."

All Liam did was reach around and stroke my other arm with his hand, knowing I wasn't done yet.

"Rayne made sure I know it's not my responsibility, and I do know. I promise." Those words sounded strangled. "But I can't let it happen to anyone else. At the same time, I can't imagine going into that room and having him look at me. Wondering if he's been imagining what he could have done if he hadn't been arrested."

Liam guided me so I was leaning farther back on the couch and he could see my face. "He can't touch you, Mara. I won't—none of us will—let that happen. And I'm still going with you, if you want me."

I did.

"It makes me sick," I said. "Having to do it. But I think it will make me sicker not to go."

"Then we'll go," he said. "And you'll be incredible."

Incredible wasn't the word I'd use to describe myself, but hearing it from him? I'd listen to that all day long.

Liam leaned in and brushed my mouth with his. A kiss not leading anywhere, but meant to soothe and comfort. I wanted to be ready for more with him. My body was definitely already there, yearning and desire rising whenever he was close.

My mind? It was almost there. And I loved Liam more because he wasn't rushing us toward anything. If anything, he was going slower than I might need. It made me smile despite the kiss.

"There you are," he whispered before kissing me again.

"You bring me back," I say.

It was his turn to smile. "And I always will. Promise."

Chapter 11

Liam

THE TRIP to Phoenix was smooth and easy, but I knew this was the simplest part of the journey.

From early this morning when Mara and I had to drive down to Missoula once again for the flight, she'd barely said a word, and I hadn't expected her to. I would always encourage her to speak, but she needed her words for the hearing tomorrow far more than I needed them today.

Mara didn't believe I was willing to do whatever she needed. Not only willing, but *happy*. This was the perfect time to show it.

"Okay," I said, taking her hand. "Let's grab the bags and the car. We can either do room service at the hotel or some kind of delivery. If you want to go out, I'm game."

She shook her head once, as I expected, and squeezed my hand. The whole flight, she'd leaned her head on my shoulder, and I fought both the physical reaction of my body and a smile so wide it made my face hurt.

Here, outside of the ranch and Montana, I was on high alert. My mind reverted to my military days. I was in full protective mode and doing my best not to show it. Jude and Daniel agreed I needed to be on the lookout.

Given the package Mara had received, and Malcolm Novic's spotless record, there was a good chance that someone was working for him on either the outside or the inside. Or both. If they were watching, I wanted to know. Allowing Mara to be in danger was not an option.

Our bags came off the carousel, and I grabbed a cart for them before heading to the car rental. It would be weird not driving a truck for the first time in years. It was also strange to be in a place that was so dry and so hot.

Montana could be hell in the summer, but it had nothing on this place.

Our hotel wasn't far from the courthouse where the hearing would take place. But far enough it allowed for some breathing room. The rooms I'd reserved were adjoining. I wasn't about to assume Mara wanted to share a room with me, but I didn't want us far apart. Just in case.

"Home sweet home." I pushed open the door to her room. "Let me go open mine, and we can open the center door."

She didn't protest, setting her bag next to the bed.

Right now? No response was a good response.

I tossed my suitcase on my bed and opened the door between our rooms and knocked on the one that led to hers. She opened it, and when I saw her face, it hit me in the gut.

Mara looked so sad and so unsure. She wanted to be here, and at the same time, she wanted to be absolutely anywhere else.

I opened my arms, and she stepped into them, burying her face in my chest. The satisfaction of knowing she felt safe enough with me was impossible to ignore. I would never take it for granted.

"How are you doing?" I asked quietly. "If you don't want to talk, tap twice, and I'll give you options."

Her fingers tapped twice gently on my back.

"All right. If one is the worst you've ever felt in your life, and ten is the best, where are you now?"

She pulled away and flashed me four fingers. Then five. Then four again. So not the best, not the worst.

It was later in the evening, because there were rarely good flight options to anywhere from Montana. "What would you like to do? I can grab us food, and we can see if there's a movie or something on TV. We can get food, and I can leave you alone to sleep. Anything you want."

Stepping up on her toes, she pressed her lips to my ear so I could hear her breathy whispers. "Food. Shower. Movie."

"We can do that. Do you have a preference for food?"

A headshake.

"Okay." I kissed her forehead. "Do what you need to do. I'll take care of it."

Before retreating, I glanced at the inside of her door. The bolts were locked. Good.

The doors between the rooms stayed open, but only a sliver so she could have some privacy. True to form, plenty of takeout brochures and a list of delivery places were in one of the drawers. I started to look through them while I called Daniel.

"You guys are there?"

"Yeah, we're in the hotel. Sorry, wanted to get Mara settled first."

Daniel's tone was careful. "How's she holding up?"

"As good as can be expected. Anything we should know?"

"No, you're in the clear. Nothing's changed. But be careful anyway."

"Always." I spread out the list of restaurants. "Let me know if anything changes."

"Will do."

I ended the call and looked up a Chinese restaurant on my phone. It looked decent, and it was hard to get good Chinese in Montana. So I put together an order as I heard the water turn on from Mara's room.

All we needed was the movie now. I didn't know what kinds of movies Mara liked—we hadn't gotten that far. I needed to ask her.

The Chinese food was fast, and I slipped down to the lobby to grab it. By the time she was out of the shower, I had an entire buffet laid out on my desk. We'd eat in here and watch in here, so at any time, she could retreat to her room and she didn't need to feel like she was kicking me out.

Mara knocked softly, her hair damp from the shower, and in soft, comfy clothes I made a point not to look at too closely. She was the sexiest woman I'd ever seen, and being so close, with wet hair…

"I—uh." I cleared my throat. "I got a bunch of food. Basically the whole menu. Whatever you want. But I wasn't sure what kind of movie you wanted."

Mara smiled and put a hand over her heart. Looking at the television, she shrugged and shook her head. She didn't care. Another time, I would pull it out of her, but tonight, I understood. She needed a distraction from tomorrow, and she didn't care what it was.

I watched her pick the food she liked, noticing the way she gravitated toward the sesame and orange chicken. The fried rice. She took some egg drop soup too. I wanted to memorize everything about her until she was all I could see and breathe.

Mara saw me staring at her and froze. Color rose to her cheeks. "Sorry," I said with a smile. "I can't stop looking at you."

She raised her eyebrows in question.

"Why?"

One nod.

"Because you're beautiful. And you're doing this even though you don't want to, and you're handling it better than I ever could."

The look she gave me said she didn't believe me at all. That was fine. She didn't need to believe it, because it was already true. Someday I hoped she would look back and be able to see it.

I didn't push her.

There was an action movie on that I'd seen a few times. Interesting enough to watch, but not something I needed to pay attention to. Mara was my real focus. She ate, and when she was finished, she curled up beside me on the bed and fell asleep.

I waited until the movie finished before I moved, lifting her up and carrying her back to her bedroom. When Mara and I truly shared a bed for the first time, I wanted her to be aware of it.

She stirred when I laid her down, but she didn't wake up. I covered her with a blanket and left the doors between our rooms cracked. Tomorrow was going to be hard for her. I only hoped I could make it better.

———

THE COURTHOUSE WAS MORE casual than I imagined it would be. The courthouses in Montana—and Missoula, especially—were older buildings with grandiose painted ceilings. It made you think the judge should be wearing a powdered wig. But the building here was closer to an office building. Big and square from the outside, bland inside.

As a much bigger city, Phoenix needed to focus on efficiency and movement. Not aesthetics.

I kept my hand on Mara's lower back as we moved through the security, only releasing her to let her go through the metal detector. She hadn't said a word all morning.

"Mara, there you are." A tall woman with blond hair approached us. "It's good to see you again. You look well."

"Thank you." Mara's first and only words of the day.

"I'm Claire Marshall." The woman held out her hand to me. "Mara's lawyer. And you are?"

I took her hand and shook it. "I'm Liam. Mara's boyfriend." It was a risk to say it, but I glanced down at Mara and took her hand. The look on her face was all I needed. She was more than happy for me to take the title. It felt like a lifetime since I'd really seen her smile.

The lawyer's eyebrows rose into her hairline. "Oh. I wasn't aware you'd be here."

Wrapping an arm around Mara's shoulders, I pulled her closer. "Just here to support Mara. I won't get in the way."

She looked me up and down, like she was doubting whether it was true. "Come on, then," she said. "We need to get to the courtroom. Things are starting shortly."

We followed Claire down the maze of twisting halls until she pushed open a set of double doors. It wasn't a typical courtroom, because instead of one judge, there was a panel of people who'd be listening. The rest of it was set up in a familiar format.

Beside me, Mara went rigid. I followed her gaze to where he sat. I'd seen a picture of him, but in the picture, he was younger. As I studied him now, in a prison jumpsuit, Malcolm Novic looked absolutely ordinary. Like many of the men who managed to con people with extreme charisma or manipulation.

Speaking to him was one thing. But looking at him was another, and he was just a man. A man who was looking over his shoulder at Mara, while she stared at him.

People sat on his side of the courtroom, and their expressions weren't friendly either. Toward both Mara and me. I wanted to protect her from their gazes, because if looks could kill…

Slipping a hand around her waist, I turned her toward me, but her eyes stayed on him. "Mara?"

She let out a shuddering breath.

"Look at me, sweetheart." Her eyes finally found mine. Everything about her was terrified. "You still with me?"

Mara swallowed. "I don't know."

"I do," I said. "You've got this."

I took her face in my hands and kissed her. The only thing I could do was be here for her.

"Mara," Claire said. "It's time."

When I released her, I smiled, but hers was nowhere to be found. I couldn't help but think it looked like she was going to her own funeral.

I found a seat, but I felt eyes on me. Malcolm Novic was looking at me, and in his eyes, I saw nothing but madness and fury.

Chapter 12

Mara

I COULDN'T BREATHE.

Letting go of Liam's hand was the hardest thing I'd ever had to do. I should be listening to what the people at the front of the room were saying, but there was a ringing in my ears, and nothing was breaking through it. Because *Malcolm* was right there.

Claire touched me on the shoulder, and I startled. She was looking at me expectantly. "What?"

"Time to go." She looked toward the front of the room, and so did I. The panels' eyes were on me. The other lawyer was looking at me. Everyone was looking at me. One of the women on the panel smiled encouragingly and gestured to the chair positioned next to the panel.

I stood.

One step at a time, Mara.

Senses. Find them.

There was a floor beneath my feet and the barest hint of

lemony scent in the air. Like a cleaning solution. In the silence, I heard the air conditioner humming. Don't look at Malcolm. Don't look at Malcolm.

Don't look at Malcolm.

Claire cleared her throat, and I looked at her. "Can you state your name for the record, please?"

I opened my mouth, and nothing came out. Closing my eyes, I took a deep breath. I could do this. I could do this. "My name is Mara Greene."

"And can you tell us why you're here?"

"I'm here because…" I curled my hands into fists. "I was in The Family. A victim of The Family."

A laugh reached my ears, and chills covered my skin. "A victim. Never." The words were so quiet I didn't know if the people on the panel had heard them. But I had. I looked straight at him.

No.

He was so much closer than when I'd entered the room. Malcolm had a smile on his face, and to anyone else, it might look like a normal, friendly smile. But I knew this man's face like my own. Every single one of us had memorized the nuances of his expressions in order to survive.

This smile was evil. In it, I saw all the plans he had for me. It was everything I'd feared. As if no time had passed since that day in his office. I could still *feel* his hand on my cheek and sense the dread in my stomach. If he had another chance to make me his bride and whore me out to all his followers, he would take it. Because that was who I was to him. It was all I'd ever been. And that didn't even scratch the surface of everything in his twisted mind. I had no doubt he had things he wanted from me that I didn't know. Sick fantasies played out with the brides of honor and the rest of the men.

And everything else?

What happened to my mother? What happened to the other women and brides who disappeared? What had they really done to them? What would they have done to me? Would I still be alive?

"Miss Greene," the woman who'd smiled on the panel spoke. "Please tell us your experience with Mr. Novic."

I felt hot, like I'd been sitting in the sun forever. A drop of sweat crept down my spine underneath my shirt. At Rayne's suggestion, I'd written down what I wanted to say, but right now, I couldn't remember any of the words.

"I—" Suddenly, I was shaking. My eyes couldn't quite focus on anything. I kept looking at Malcolm and Claire, and I knew what I needed to say. I knew. "I was—"

"Maybe I should speak first," Malcolm said. "Give her a chance to get her story straight in her head."

"No," I gasped out. "No."

"Mr. Novic, you will have your turn."

I shook my head. "He wanted to…" My throat closed up. I couldn't even draw a breath.

"We were pressured into a public proceeding to allow for witness statements," Malcolm's lawyer said. "And this witness can't manage to say anything? This is a waste of everyone's time. I agree we should move on to my client's testimony and reach the decision quickly."

Sickness bubbled in my gut. This wasn't the way this was supposed to go. I needed to do this. I needed to tell them the truth.

"Mr. Novic—"

"No, you're right," he said. "My apologies, of course. We should wait and hear what *Mara* has to say. I'm sure it will be illuminating. That is her name, right? Mara?"

"Miss Greene." Claire's voice cut through everything, and I managed to look at her. "When did you join The Family?"

Questions. I could answer questions. Maybe. "Six. I was six."

"And what happened when you were fifteen?"

"Don't lead her," Malcolm's lawyer snapped.

"He tried to…" I looked at him, and his smile was as wide as it could be. My mind flooded with memories. The same smile he had when he'd married Adrian. Before she came back with bruises and a broken gaze. The same one he had when he'd seen me in the mockup of the wedding dress they were making for me.

The same smile he had when he'd told me my mother was gone, but he'd always take care of me. He held me too close and for too long, and I didn't dare move until he did.

Liam snapped into focus, his eyes on mine. He looked worried. I just needed to open my mouth and *speak*.

Sickness swirled again, and I couldn't. If I opened my mouth right now, I was going to throw up all over the room. Bile burned at the back of my tongue.

"Miss Greene?" the woman asked. "We need to hear from you, please."

Tears blurred my eyes. Every bit of work I'd done to get to this point was gone. I couldn't even conjure my voice when I was in the same place as him. He would win, and I'd failed. I'd come here for nothing.

"I—"

Terror and nausea spiraled through me like a tornado. I was on my feet and moving before I fully registered that I *was* moving.

"*Miss Greene.*"

"Mr. Novic was clearly taunting my client. A victim. She shouldn't have to be put on display—"

Claire's voice cut off as I pushed open the doors and ran. Bathroom. There was the bathroom. I'd seen it on the way in, and I sprinted for it. Saliva coated my mouth, and I only had seconds. Straight for the biggest stall, I didn't even lock it behind me, hitting my knees and emptying my stomach.

I hadn't eaten anything this morning, but it didn't matter. My body wanted to be empty. Empty of food, memories, emotions, anything that would root me here to this moment. I never should have come here. No matter what kinds of noble aims I'd had, I should have known I wasn't ready.

Wasn't good enough.

Tears were streaming down my face, and as I came down, I could hear myself sobbing, the awful sounds of heaving echoing off the walls.

"Mara?" Liam's voice filled the bathroom.

His hands brushed down my spine and pulled back my hair. "You're all right," he said. "You're okay. You're safe."

I spat into the toilet and flushed it. My body was empty for now, but I felt so sick, my body aching, weak enough that I was shaking. "I can go back in," I said weakly.

The truth was, I wasn't sure. But we'd come all this way, and I was such a failure… I didn't want it to end like this. Liam shook his head. "The lawyers were arguing. They sent him back to prison and postponed everything. The panel wants to talk it over."

"Because of me?"

He was crouched in front of me. "They didn't say. All they said was they needed time to reassess things."

I looked down. "Okay."

It wasn't okay. None of this was okay. But what else was there to do?

"Let's get out of here," Liam said. "Are you okay to stand?"

I took his hand, and it was mostly his strength lifting me up. Quickly, I went to the sink and rinsed out my mouth. It was still gross, but better.

Liam was with me as I stepped out, and Claire was there

waiting. She looked resigned. "You told me you were ready, Mara." Her voice wasn't unkind, but neither was it sympathetic.

I shook my head. How did I tell her I thought I'd been ready? I really did think I was, and I'd never been more wrong.

"We'll see. His lawyer might try to spin this as a way to ensure his release. Like we were stalling. Just throwing false things at them to keep him in prison."

"What?" Liam said. "That isn't what happened, and it was pretty clear."

"Clear doesn't mean anything in situations like these."

"They should see a woman, who has detailed history with the man, unable to speak. Because of what *he* did. Not anything else."

Claire was glaring at Liam. "I agree. But just because it's what they *should* see doesn't mean it's what they *will* see. And right now, it's a coin flip about what they'll decide. But I guess I'll let you know."

She turned and started walking away.

"I'm sorry."

When she turned, her face was a little softer. "I know you are."

She disappeared around a corner, and I sighed. I was uncomfortable in my own skin. Everything I'd been afraid of had happened. The only good thing was that, for the moment, Malcolm was still in prison. But it wasn't a guarantee, and even my lawyer was disappointed in me.

Malcolm was probably over the moon. It didn't make me feel any better.

Liam pulled me close and kissed my temple. "Let's go," he said quietly. "You don't need to stay here anymore."

He was right. We didn't need to stay here. I wasn't doing anyone any good anyway.

———

I WENT STRAIGHT into my room when we got back to the hotel. The doors between the rooms were shut because of Liam and me getting dressed this morning, and I didn't open mine.

Instead, I curled up on the bed and stared at the wall. Liam told me he was there for whatever I needed, but I didn't know what I needed.

All I felt was failure. The one thing I could do to help, and I didn't do it. So much worse than it had been before. I barely remembered the first time in court with Malcolm. I only had impressions of fear, brightness, and urgency.

In front of me, I saw only a spiral aiming downward. I needed everything and nothing. But I couldn't be alone, even if I couldn't speak. Of all the people in the world, I knew Liam would never shame me for not being able to speak. But by the same token, talking was easier with him.

Forcing myself up off the bed, I changed into the pajamas I'd brought with me before approaching the door. I shouldn't be nervous about it. This was *Liam*. But I was nervous about everything right now.

I knocked on the door and heard the gentle shuffle of movement on the other side. Liam opened his side and smiled. He was comfortable now too, in sweats and a T-shirt, and no part of him looked disappointed or upset.

"Hey."

"Hi." My throat felt scratchy, and I wrapped my arms around myself.

Liam stuck his hands in the pockets of his sweatpants, and I could look at him like this forever. Just like he'd said to me last night. I'd barely been able to think or breathe, and I'd been confused when I'd woken up in my hotel room instead of his.

He took a step forward and looked at me. "Do you feel like talking?"

I shook my head.

"You want options?"

Relief swept through me.

"Okay." He came and wrapped his arms around me. "One tap if you want to get food. Two taps if you just want to relax for a while. Three taps if you want me to distract you with something, whether it's a movie or anything else."

One breath in, and one breath out. I tapped twice.

"Okay. We can do that," he said. And without another word, he picked me up and carried me to my bed, still freshly made from housekeeping.

Liam curved himself behind me, one arm around my waist. "Is this all right?"

I nodded. Having Liam close was calming, and I curled in on myself further.

Slowly, my body relaxed. Tension released I hadn't even realized I was clinging to.

"If you don't want to talk, it's all right," he said quietly. "But I still want you to know how proud I am of you."

A sob broke out of me. "Don't be."

"Why not?"

"I ruined it," I whispered. "I couldn't get him out of my head. Everything he did—I needed to tell them, and I failed."

"I don't see it that way."

I closed my eyes. "I'm not sure there's another way to see it."

"Will you let me see *you*?"

Slowly, I turned in his arms until I was facing him. I couldn't meet his eyes. But he could see me.

"The way I see it," he said. "Is you came down here to do the right thing. You came down here to make sure no

112

one else had to go through anything like what you went through. You didn't want to, but you still did it, because protecting other people was more important to you than anything else.

"It's been a long time since you've seen him, and he was toying with you."

"Was he?"

"*Yes*." Liam's voice was firm. "If the panel can't see that, they shouldn't be allowed to make those kinds of decisions. Good behavior or not, he was out of line. I saw the way he looked at you."

"Well," I sighed. "It worked. He won."

"We don't know that yet. They're going to review things. You couldn't see yourself, but I did. Nothing about you said you were faking it, Mara. The only thing there was to see was a woman who had *too much* to say."

I smiled once and let it drop.

"You don't believe me."

"It's hard."

A kiss warmed my forehead. "I hope someday you'll be able to see how strong you are. Because I see it. I feel it."

Breathing out, I leaned my head against him. "I feel it more when I'm with you. Even if I shouldn't."

"Why shouldn't you?"

"Because I don't want to use you as a crutch. You deserve better than that."

Liam pulled me away from him just far enough so I could see his face, lifting my chin so I was looking at him and his gorgeous brown eyes. "Would you need crutches if you broke your leg?"

"Of course."

"But crutches aren't the only things that help you heal. They're just one of the tools. You have the cast and boot, the doctor's appointments. Making sure you get enough rest.

And when you've healed enough, you don't need the crutches anymore."

I shook my head. "That's why you can't be one. I—"

My voice stopped, and Liam smiled like he knew what I was going to say and didn't. "I'm not going anywhere," he said. "I promise. And I don't mind if I'm part of helping you heal. I would love that. But what I want more is for you to be happy and feel safe. For you to be able to leave this in the past, if that's where you want it. I'll be as big or as little a part of that journey as you want me to be."

We settled into silence for a while, and I enjoyed the sensation of Liam's hands moving up and down my spine. I wanted more than this with him. So much more. But tonight wasn't the night. As much as I wanted it, I didn't want any of our firsts to be tainted by Malcolm.

"I'm sorry we had to come all the way down here for nothing."

"I'm not. We got to spend time together."

I laughed, and it felt good. "Me being a complete mess and silent?"

Liam grinned too. "Even when you're not talking, you're speaking. You say everything with your eyes."

This was what I wanted. Ease and comfort. At some point, we would probably be hungry, but right now, I didn't want to move. "Tell me something," I whispered. "A good story or memory." Anything that didn't have to do with me and The Family.

"Hmm. Let's see. I grew up in California." I blinked in surprise, and he chuckled. "I know. That's the reaction I get most of the time. But I never really fit in there. It was too crowded and too loud. Montana is much better."

"You were a beach boy. Now I understand why you were a SEAL."

"That was part of it," he admitted. "But not all of it.

That's a story for a different time. This story is about the time I decided to run away."

I smiled and settled in to listen.

"I'd seen some people living on the beach, and I never wanted to leave the ocean. So when I was ten, I decided I was going to run away and live on the beach. I actually got all the way there, ready to start my brand-new life as a bum in the sun. Unluckily for me, my favorite place wasn't a secret. My family found me and brought me back before dinnertime. Sometimes I still wish I could go spend some time on the beach, but I've learned to love the mountains. And what the mountains gave me."

My face asked the question, and I flushed when he just grinned. *Me.* The mountains gave him me.

"Now I want you to tell me something," he said. "I want to know about your tattoos."

"What about them?"

"I'm just curious what they're for and why you got them. I'm especially curious about the one on your back. I've only ever seen a little piece of it."

Heat curled deep inside me, pleased he wanted to see it. "When I started working with Rayne, one of the first things we did was work on ways I could reclaim things. She didn't pressure me or give me the idea, but we did talk about it. I wanted to put something on my body *I* wanted to be there.

"The only marks I'd ever had on my body were when they beat me. This was still pain, but it was pain I chose."

The anger in Liam's eyes was pure fire. I wished I could see him unleashed on Malcolm. There wouldn't be a contest.

"And the one on your back?"

I cleared my throat. "A hawk. I know I said I wanted to be a cat, but I like birds too. They're free. They never have to worry about being locked anywhere, when they can just fly away. And I liked the idea of being both free and feared."

Awe entered Liam's face. He'd had no way of knowing what my tattoo was when he said he'd be a bird of prey. But I knew, and it had felt too perfect at the time to say anything.

"Your turn," I said. "More stories."

"Right," he said, brushing the hair out of my face. "More stories."

Liam kept talking, and I sank into the sound of his voice. For tonight, I would take all the comfort he was offering me and not worry about anything else but him and me.

It was far too early to sleep, but I found myself drifting with a smile on my face. This was a feeling I wanted forever, and the deepest part of me hoped Liam would always be the one to make it possible.

Chapter 13

Liam

MARA FELL asleep in my arms, and no chance in hell was I moving away from her. She was easy to hold, and with her by my side, I could relax.

Arizona's bright sun peeking through the drapes woke me early. Mara had turned in her sleep, curling into my chest. She was lying across me, hand touching my ribs, and I couldn't stop the smile on my face.

Her body was relaxed and easy against mine. Maybe the most relaxed I'd ever seen or felt. The man in me desperately wanted to be the reason for her comfort and relaxation, but she was sleeping, and it was probably that alone.

Moving slowly enough I didn't wake her, I gently eased Mara down onto the pillows and off my body. She barely stirred. Unsurprising, given yesterday. Even agreeing to come down here had been stressful.

I checked the locks once more before returning to my room, leaving the doors between them cracked. Our flight wasn't until this afternoon, but I'd never broken the habit of waking up at dawn. Years of training that went so deep I couldn't shake it.

A quick shower and I was refreshed. We hadn't brought much with us, and my suitcase was packed in minutes. One glance through the door showed me Mara was still deeply asleep. I wasn't about to interrupt her. But I could surprise her when she woke.

I wrote a quick note on the hotel's paper in case she did wake up and left it on the nightstand beside her. We needed coffee and breakfast. I remembered a coffee shop not far from here we passed yesterday on the way to the courthouse.

Using the door in my room to make sure I was quiet, I slipped out.

Even though autumn was close, it was already warm this early in the morning. There was no way I could live in this kind of heat all the time. The days when I'd lived in the California heat I'd told Mara about seemed very far away, and now that I'd experienced the cold of Montana, there was no way to go back.

The coffee shop bustled with morning commuters, and I found myself watching people out of curiosity. Clocking faces and marking them out of habit. A couple of the people in the coffee shop looked familiar, but given our proximity to the courthouse, that wasn't strange.

I pulled out my phone while I waited and called the ranch to check in. "Hey."

"Hey," Daniel said. "How'd it go?"

I laughed, but there was nothing funny about this. "I'm having a hard time thinking of a way it could have gone worse."

"Shit." The word was said under his breath. "I'm sorry. Is Mara okay?"

Mara's trauma wasn't mine to share, but this was pretty

clear. "No, she's not. Don't know what's going to happen in terms of the hearing yet. We'll have to wait and see. Either way, we're home this evening."

"Okay. We'll see you when you get here. As far as I'm concerned, you're covered until this is over. Do what you need to do, and we have the rest. For both of you."

"I appreciate it."

"Where are you right now?"

"Grabbing breakfast," I said. "After everything yesterday, we hunkered down."

Daniel made a sound of acknowledgment, and I could almost see him nodding. It was good that everyone understood and was supportive. It made this easier. "Let us know when you land."

I hung up and stepped up to the counter.

Just like with the Chinese food, I wasn't sure what Mara liked or ate for breakfast. So I ordered a bunch of things, making everyone in line behind me hate my guts. More than one movie I remembered had a scene just like it.

Smiling to myself, I pretended not to notice. Mara was worth whatever frustration people had at me, and I left a good tip for the baristas. I knew how hard Lena worked at Deja Brew, and the people here were no exception.

I ended up with four drinks and a bag of pastries that looked like I was buying food for an entire office. There was a nearly audible sigh of relief as I stepped out of the way, and I smiled. They were never going to see me again anyway.

Despite the crowd in the coffee shop, the sidewalk was almost entirely empty this early. If I was lucky, Mara would still be asleep when I got back, and I would get to be with her when she woke.

Blowing out a breath, I steadied myself. It was way too soon for me to be thinking about waking up every day with her, but my mind didn't agree. It was *all* I could think about. Gorgeous blue eyes opening and meeting mine, both sleepy and happy? It sounded like heaven.

Air moved, and I sensed the impact a second before I felt it.

A body slammed into mine, taking me into the alley next to me. I hit the wall hard. Pain ruptured through my arm, and again where the assailant was punching me.

Assess.

More than one person was around me. They wore masks to hide their identities. Three of them and two in waiting? This was an ambush.

Defend.

My mind still reeled from the first hit, but it didn't matter. I'd dealt with more pain than this. Another hit came, and I ducked underneath it. Backed against the wall wasn't the ideal way to fight, but I didn't have to worry about anyone behind me.

I caught a foot before it connected with my ribs and shoved it away, but they were coming all at once. My head snapped to the side, and fire flashed behind my eyes.

Fuck.

Lucky punch.

One of them had a bat. If I got hit with that, it could do some serious damage.

Turning off my mind, I let loose, going to a place where survival was the only goal. I shoved the attacker in front of me across the alley and used the momentum, carrying him into the opposite wall and hitting him three times in rapid succession. Fast enough that the other two barely had time to register.

I dropped the now-unconscious man and turned, ducking under the swing of the bat and knocking it in the same direction so it flew out of his hands. And I ran.

Ninety percent of the time, the most important thing in any combat situation was survival. I ran past the mess of coffee and food on the ground and straight to the hotel. Only once did I look back, and they weren't following. They had some combat skills, but the way they'd jumped me, I doubted they were expecting me to fight back. They were less concerned with me and more concerned with the one I'd knocked out.

In the lobby, I slowed down only to make sure the staff didn't panic. Though, looking the way I did—with blood dripping down my face—I probably still appeared out of my mind.

Not bothering with the elevator, I sprinted up the stairs two at a time. Everything in me needed to get back to Mara. I didn't believe in coincidences, and getting jumped the day after what had happened in the courtroom? It felt convenient.

Mara might not have seen the way Malcolm's followers were looking at both her and me, but I had. Combine it with receiving the veil, and then this? It added up to someone trying to terrify and isolate her. On top of it all, if they knew where I was, they knew where *she* was.

I unlocked the door to my room and opened it as quietly as I could. Nothing looked amiss, and a second later, I heard the shower in Mara's room.

After checking to make sure her room was, in fact, empty, I retreated and sat on my bed, catching my breath. They'd gotten a few good shots in while I was disoriented. I would have some bruises on my ribs, but it could have been much worse. My head could be cracked open with a bat right now, and Mara would be alone.

In the mirror, I saw the nasty cut on my cheek. Bastard must have had something on his knuckles. But it would be fine once I cleaned it.

The shower shut off, and I took a painful breath. I needed to report this, but I also didn't want Mara to hear me talking to the cops before I had time to tell her and show her.

When I heard the bathroom door open, I called to her. "Mara? I'm back."

"Okay." Her voice was soft.

"Something happened. I'm okay, so please don't panic."

The silence in the air became acute.

I tracked her quiet footsteps to the doors between the rooms, and she pushed them open, wrapped in nothing but a towel. Her eyes went wide. "Liam."

Standing, I caught her in her rush to me. "What—wh—" Her words ended in breathless nothing. Too much. It was too much.

"It's all right," I said. "I'm okay. Some bruises and this thing on my face."

"But…"

I wrapped my arms fully around her, guiding her face into my chest, where she relaxed. "I went to get us breakfast. They jumped me on the way back and didn't get far."

"Who?"

"I'm not sure," I said. "But I need to call the police and report it. Then we need to get to the airport. No way in hell we're staying here longer than we have to."

She nodded, holding me tighter.

Guilt flowed through me. This was the last thing she needed. "I'll call the police while you get dressed and pack," I said quietly before I pulled her away from me, solely so I could kiss her.

It wasn't lost on me that she was only in a towel, and despite it being the worst timing in the world, I was only so strong. Her eyes were glassy when we broke apart. "I promise I'm okay, sweetheart. I promise."

She pointed at herself, and there was a question in her eyes. Was this because of her?

"Do I think it was random? No. Malcolm had some people with him in court yesterday that were giving me nasty looks. But no matter what, it has absolutely nothing to do with you." She was already shaking her head, and I didn't let her, cupping her face with my hands. "You are never responsible for someone else's choice of violence, okay?"

"Okay." I hated how small she sounded, so I kissed her one more time the way I really wanted to, until I felt her relax once more.

She didn't want to step away from me, and I didn't want to let her go. As soon as I could, I would have her in my arms again.

I dialed the police.

"Nine-one-one, what is your emergency?"

"I was just attacked," I told the dispatcher. "Jumped by some masked men on the street."

"Are you currently safe?"

Was I safe? Were *we* safe? I didn't know. But that wasn't what she was asking. "Yes. I managed to get away and return to my hotel."

"What is your current location?"

I gave her the hotel's address and more details about the attack. When I ended the call, the police were on their way. The front desk needed to know as well. Otherwise, they were going to freak out when police came into the hotel. They agreed to bring up a first aid kit after I called.

Not even ten minutes later, Mara was dressed and packed. I put our suitcases by the door and double-checked before opening the door to the hotel employee with the first aid kit. Mara grabbed it and grabbed me, sitting me down on the bed.

The kit was open, and she was going through it with hands that were way too skilled with the bare-bones supplies.

She reached for me, holding my face still as she cleaned the cut so gently I barely felt it. "Mara?"

No response. All of her was wrapped up in the singular focus of fixing me. A bandage she placed *did* make the wound feel better.

But while she was putting everything back into the box, Mara was distinctly avoiding my eyes.

"Sweetheart, will you look at me?"

Finally, she did, and I didn't like what I saw there. Sadness and insecurity. Thankfully, I knew none of those emotions had to do with me. "You helped other people with injuries like this?"

She nodded.

"Thank you for helping me."

I pulled her closer and savored the feeling of her while we waited, and the knock came far too soon.

"Phoenix Police."

We opened the door, and the two police officers took in the bandage on my face and the state of my clothes. "You're Liam Anderson?"

"I am. Please, come in."

The next hour was a whirlwind of telling the police what had happened, showing them where it had happened, and relaying why we were in Phoenix. Through it all, Mara stayed by my side, and there wasn't a moment we weren't touching, whether that was holding hands or my arm around her waist.

Now we were once more in the hotel room, finishing things. We needed to head to the airport soon.

"I wish I could say this was uncommon, Mr. Anderson, but it happens. It's more likely it was a random act of violence and nothing to do with your court case."

I looked between the officers. "Are you familiar with The Family?"

"We are," the other one said. "Or at least, we're aware of them. But there haven't been any problems with their members in years, and when their leader is about to get out? It doesn't make sense for them to endanger that."

The first officer winced. "And we don't have any proof it was them."

"I understand." I wasn't convinced, but I understood.

"We have your information, and we'll check cameras and anything else we can find and let you know, okay?"

I nodded and stood, shaking hands with the man. "I look forward to hearing from you."

We both waited until they closed the door behind them before I wrapped her up again. "Ready to go home?"

Mara blew out a shaky breath. "Yes, please."

And we did. We didn't exchange many words as we went to the airport and flew back to Montana. Nor were there many on the drive back to the ranch, but there didn't need to be. The closer we got to home, the better I felt and the better Mara looked.

Yet I couldn't imagine just leaving her at her house and driving away. Not after everything.

We pulled up to her cabin as the sun met the horizon. "Mara," I said, looking over at her.

She looked at me, and I was soothed by the hope in her eyes.

"Would it be too much if I told you I wasn't ready to let you go?"

"I didn't want to ask," she whispered.

"You can *always* ask," I told her. "Anything. If you have to whisper it, write it down, shout it from the fucking rooftops. You never have to hide anything from me."

Mara smiled. It was the first one I'd seen all day. "Yeah. Going to take some practice."

I pulled her across the seat and kissed her temple. "So, I can take you home with me?"

"Yes. I need to get some new clothes."

"And I need to talk to the guys about what happened. Just outside, if that's okay."

She nodded, and I grabbed her suitcase out of the back of the truck, carrying it to the house for her. We took pains to make sure the property was safe, but I still looked around the open space before I stepped back outside. "Take as long as you need."

She left the door open, taking the suitcase all the way inside.

Daniel answered my call on the first ring. "We're home," I told him. "We need to talk. Whoever's around, can you drive down to Mara's? I don't want to leave her."

"We'll be right there."

A few minutes later, dust flew up behind Daniel's truck as it came rushing to a stop in front of Mara's house. Lucas and Daniel climbed out of the front seats while Jude and Noah jumped out of the back.

Jude looked me up and down. "What the hell happened to you?"

After hours of shoving it down, I finally let some of the anger and frustration surface. "I got jumped. Out of nowhere. Three guys. They ambushed me, and the cops are looking, but I'm not optimistic. They were careful."

"You think it was The Family?"

"Yes. The way they looked at me yesterday? And I don't mean just the asshole who's in jail. It was like anyone being with Mara at all was the worst thing imaginable."

Daniel ran a hand over his face. "Well, this changes things. It could be more dangerous than we thought."

"Things are starting to add up." I shook my head. "I'm terrified for her."

Lucas shot me a wan smile. "Welcome to the club. We should get jackets."

"We'll dig into it." Jude crossed his arms and nodded. "If they're coming after *our* family, they have another thing coming."

"Thank you." I looked at each of them. "Seriously."

Noah clapped me on the shoulder. "You don't need to thank us, Liam. We protect our family. You and Mara are both part of it." He took a breath. "And you've risked a lot for all of us."

The night Noah and I had almost died was close in my mind. We'd been lucky. There wasn't any other way to spin it. Hopefully we wouldn't be in that situation again, but I knew if someone tried to hurt Mara? I wouldn't hesitate, and they wouldn't either.

"I know I don't have to say it, but I still will. Thank you."

Behind me, the door shut. Mara stood at the door and looked at me with her suitcase in hand. Even from here, I saw her blush. Because they knew she was coming home with me. But she didn't shy away from it either. We were in this together now.

"Have a good night, Liam," Daniel said. "Get some rest. We'll let you know if we find anything."

I nodded, and they drove away while I got Mara's suitcase back into the truck. It was time to go home.

Chapter 14

Mara

SILENCE.

It was what surrounded us as we drove away from the ranch. We'd been quiet all day, but this felt different. Liam spoke when he needed to, but now, he said nothing.

I glanced over at him, trying to figure out whether he was in pain because of this morning. He hadn't shown any signs of it, but what he told the police officers sounded far more brutal than I'd imagined. And it was my fault.

He could tell me it wasn't all he wanted, but Liam wouldn't have been in Phoenix if it weren't for me. He wouldn't have a target on his back. Hell, he wouldn't have gone out for coffee.

Gritting my teeth, I closed my eyes and tried to focus on what he'd said. I wasn't responsible for anyone else's violence. That lie was difficult to untangle.

My entire existence had been trying to prevent violence with my actions. If I wasn't good enough, if I didn't do enough, then it was my fault, and I needed punishment. Seeing Malcolm brought all of it back to the surface.

None of it was true.

I was so desperately tired of having to unravel the lie over and over and over, but it also wasn't going to stop. Like Rayne said, recovery wasn't a straightforward process, no matter how much I wished it were.

We pulled up to a house on the far side of Garnet Bend. There were other houses nearby, but not next door. It seemed like each house had a large chunk of land to go with it. It was a perfect, lovely neighborhood. I didn't spend much time in the residential sections of the town, but this was so pretty.

Several large trees overshadowed the two-story house, painted a dark red that looked vibrant without being overkill. It was a good size, and most of all, I couldn't help but think this wasn't the kind of place I'd imagined Liam living.

He pulled up and shut off the engine. An unspoken tension filled the air. Not bad exactly, but not the same comfort we'd had in our silence up until now.

Liam came around the truck and helped me down, holding my hand before he got our suitcases. It was after he shut the tailgate that he sighed and looked at me. "I—" Liam swallowed.

Was he nervous?

"I don't bring a lot of people here," he said quietly. "Daniel's been here once, but the rest of the guys never have. Nor anybody else. I just—" He glanced away from me. "I hope you like it."

I touched his arm—would have hugged him if he hadn't had suitcases in both hands. We went through the front door, which was equipped with a code lock. There was also a small black screen, and Liam put down his suitcase just long enough to press his thumb to it.

Liam made me feel safe, regardless, but given what had happened this morning, I was grateful for the extra security.

He gestured for me to go first.

The house was…

It was beautiful.

Dark and shining hardwoods rolled out in front of me, complementing walls of warmer neutrals. I saw a living room that was cozy, with a couch you could sink into and an equally cozy chair that looked big enough for both of us together.

Shelves full of books graced the walls, and there was art too. I wandered into the kitchen and found it open and friendly, with enough equipment on the counters to tell me Liam cooked regularly.

The house was *warm*. Lived-in. A stack of mail sat on the counter, and a cup was by the sink. Pictures sat on the shelves with the books, and a soft blanket was slung over the back of the couch.

This was a home.

Not of the Liam everyone knew at the ranch, the quirky jokester who made everyone laugh.

This was the home of Liam the man. The person who saw me for who I was and wasn't daunted by everything that held me in its fist. The man who had taken a beating for me and held my hair back while I threw up.

Behind me, the front door shut softly, and I realized he'd hung back and waited for me to come in and see it. He was nervous. I'd never seen him act like this. This was important to him.

Liam leaned against the front door, and I walked all the way back until my body was pressed against his. My voice had mostly disappeared, but I would find it for this. When we were alone, it was always easier.

"Were you afraid to show me your home?"

He blew out a breath. "Yes."

"Why?" I wrapped my arms around his waist and leaned my head on his chest. "It's beautiful. Warm. Comfortable."

Liam's arms came around me so quick and tight, I lost my breath. "Thank you."

"I want to know why," I said. "Did you think I wouldn't like it?"

"It's not that…" He tugged me into the living room and sat in the overstuffed chair, pulling me down to sit across his lap. "Home is a difficult concept for me to begin with. I'm very protective of it."

The last of the Montana light shone through the windows, and in the orange glow, he was so handsome I wanted to take a picture. Savor this moment, because it felt like *more* than words we were speaking. "Does it have something to do with you running away?"

"Yes and no," he admitted. "I told you my family came and found me. What I didn't mention was that it was my foster family."

I said nothing, waiting for him to continue. He'd briefly mentioned being a foster child when he'd held me at the wedding.

"My parents left me when I was a baby. I never knew them, and I still don't know why, or if anything happened to them. So I grew up in the system. Nowhere permanent.

"It was one of the reasons I joined NROTC and the Navy. The idea of a team who would always have your back? I never had that, and it was everything I ever wanted."

"That does sound nice."

"While I was in the NROTC, right before I went to BUD/S, I met someone. Her name was Jenny."

I looked inside myself for some sign of jealousy and found nothing. This was clearly his past, and nothing to do with us.

"We fell in love hard and fast, and a few months later, we were married."

"I didn't know you were married." Shock colored my tone even though I tried to keep it steady.

Liam smiled sadly and squeezed my hip where his hand rested, moving it to dance slowly up and down my spine. "I'm not anymore. Being married to someone in the military is hard, and a SEAL? Even harder. But we were happy for a while. Still, I deployed, and it was difficult for her."

He swallowed and looked away. "When I came back, injured and discharged, she wasn't there. There were divorce papers on the kitchen counter."

"*What?*"

"I don't blame her. She didn't know what she was signing up for."

Anger grew under my skin. "That doesn't make it okay, and I don't buy it. It's not like you hid your career from her."

"No, I guess not," he said with a shrug. "But it was a long time ago."

As we sat, I put things together. He protected his home because he'd never had one. Sought out a brotherhood he could rely on, but it still wasn't a permanent *place*. Then the one person he thought he could count on—who was with him for life—abandoned him when it mattered the most.

Just like his family had.

No wonder this place was so important to him. The care and love he put into it was everywhere. You could *feel* it in the air.

"I understand," I said, whispering, so I didn't break the spell in the darkening quiet. "I never had a real home either until the cabin at the ranch. Before that, I was moving around, trying to find somewhere I felt safe. And with The Family…nothing really belonged to *me*."

He held me closer, and I breathed him in. Cedar and

spices. Slowly, Liam's hand moved all the way up my spine until it was buried in my hair. This was the first moment since this morning when everything was still and nothing was between us.

"I'm sorry," I finally said, barely a breath. Where my head rested on his shoulder, I was glad he couldn't see my face. "I know you told me it's not my fault, and I understand. But you were still there for me. You got hurt because you were with me."

"I got hurt because assholes decided it was a good idea to attack me. Nothing more and nothing less. If you need to hear me say I forgive you, I'll say it freely, but Mara—" he turned my face up to his "—you didn't do this."

"What if it doesn't stop? What if it really was them and they find you or me again? Someone knows I live at the ranch. What if—"

Liam kissed me, short-circuiting all the words I had in my head. This time, it wasn't because I couldn't bear to speak. They were just gone, evaporated in the heat between our bodies.

When he pulled away, I felt like I'd run a mile. My heart pounded in my ears, and my breath came in gasps.

"The guys are digging deeper to see what they can find. And if what you said happens? We'll deal with it. I'm not going anywhere, and I'm not going to let anything happen to you."

"I don't want you to get hurt again."

Leaning in until our foreheads touched, Liam met my gaze. "I would take today's injuries a hundred times, or worse, to make sure you're safe. All I thought about was getting back to you and making sure *you* were safe. I've had much worse." He kissed my cheek.

"Telling me you've had worse doesn't make me feel better."

He laughed. "Sorry. Are you hungry?" Lifting us up together, he set me on my feet and began to turn on the lights. Just like everything else, the lamps and lights made the place cozy and comfortable.

"Yes," I said, and my stomach grumbled like he'd asked it the question.

The airport was the last time I ate, and suddenly, being home and away from everything hanging over our heads unlocked my appetite.

"We can order in, or I can poke around and see what I have in the kitchen."

"Let's cook something," I said with a smile. My secret motivation was I desperately wanted to see Liam at home in his own environment.

A high bar sat behind one counter with stools, and Liam parked me there. "Something to drink?"

"I can help."

"Stay there." He pointed, and I let myself fall back onto the stool. "My house, my treat."

The face I made had him grinning. This, I loved. This was comfortable and easy. This was what life *should* be. Not worrying about the past or rehashing things you couldn't change.

Easier said than done.

I drank a cup of tea while Liam made us some pasta. Simple, but I didn't care. We were eating together, and it was delicious. Hungry as I was, I wanted the company far more than I wanted the food.

When I stood to take my plate to the sink, he stole it from me and brought it over instead. I looked at him. "You have to let me help sometime."

His eyes sparkled. "Do I?"

"*Yes*," I insisted. "You can't do everything all the time. That's not fair."

"I get to hear you speak, sweetheart. It's more than enough motivation."

I flushed scarlet, and he pretended not to notice.

"Let me get our suitcases upstairs."

Following him, I felt nerves jittering in my stomach. This was all new territory for me. He set his suitcase down by one door and carried mine to another. My feet were frozen at the top of the stairs, watching the distance between the two and questioning everything.

Liam looked over his shoulder at me and saw me waiting. I shook my head, words evaporating. How did I ask for this? Or voice the fear that was coursing through my veins with my beating heart.

The man in front of me would never know how grateful I was that he could read me, because he came back, my suitcase still with him, and stood in front of me.

"Are you all right?"

I blinked, unsure where my words went, but very sure they were gone.

Setting down the suitcase, he pulled me closer. "Tap twice for yes, sweetheart, because I hate that look in your eyes. You're scared?"

Two taps.

His words were slow and hesitant. "Are you scared of me?"

One tap. No. I couldn't even imagine being afraid of him.

A relieved smile appeared on his face. "Are you scared of being alone?"

I didn't tap. I held my hand flat and moved it back and forth. A little. I was. But it wasn't the thing at the top of my mind right now. He wasn't going to guess this.

Placing my hand on his chest, I took a long breath and

closed my eyes. Words were hard to find like this. Words made things happen, and they weren't always good.

But Liam was safe.

"I'm afraid you...don't want me."

"*Mara.*" My name was a gasp and a plea. "No."

So fast I barely caught it, I was gently pressed against the wall, his lips on mine. "I think how much I want you might scare you more," he said. "I didn't want to assume anything or make you feel pressured. But never doubt how much I want you."

Nodding, I slid my hands up his chest. This wasn't an area I had experience in, and Liam was the first person who made me want to try.

"Thank you," I whispered. "But I want to be with you."

Liam kissed me again, softer this time, before he picked up my suitcase and carried it into his bedroom.

I followed him.

Chapter 15

Mara

LIAM'S BEDROOM, like the rest of the house, was lovely. More rich, dark woods, and a bed that went on for miles. Covered in a soft comforter and plenty of pillows, it put my own bed to shame.

Setting our suitcases at the end of the bed, Liam took my hand. "Again, just because you're in here with me, I don't want you to feel pressure."

It wasn't pressure I felt. It was nerves. Being together? I wanted it, but I…

He sat on the edge of the bed, and I went with him. Saying this out loud—truly out loud—wasn't possible. But there was no way for me to tell him this without words.

As I stood between his knees, he watched me carefully. "That's a look I haven't seen before."

I leaned in to his ear so I could whisper. "I've…never…."

Liam gripped my arms and pulled me back to look at

him. He searched my face, but his expression was even. No signs of horror or disgust, just gentle curiosity. "It makes me sad to think you've never had anyone close enough to you," he said. "But given what I know about The Family, it makes sense. Which is why we don't have to rush this."

Resolve hardened in me. The Family had controlled my life long enough, and the fear of the unknown held me back from too many things. This was not one of them. Yes, nerves skittered along my spine, but if there was anyone I wanted to try and learn and fail with, it was Liam.

So I leaned forward again. "Show me," I whispered. "Teach me."

The way he held me said so much more than words. "Are you sure?"

I nodded. "Yes."

"If you change your mind, tell me, sweetheart. Nothing bad will happen. I won't be angry or disappointed. Okay?"

That was the reason I wanted him. So many other reasons, too, but he would listen to me and love me in a way that was safe. "Okay."

Liam smiled with me. "We're going slow. The rest can come later."

Reaching up, he pulled the T-shirt he was wearing over his head. During the summer, the men on the ranch sometimes lost their shirts. It wasn't an uncommon sight. But this up close and personal felt different. Liam lifted my wrists and put them on his shoulders. "You can touch me wherever and however you like, Mara."

By letting me touch him first, he gave me power. So much would be new, but he offered his own vulnerability first.

Over his ribs, I saw the bruises from this morning. Darker marks on his dark skin, and I touched them gently. Liam placed his hand over mine. "Just bruises. Not serious."

It could have been so much worse. For the moment, I put it aside. Now was not the time for it. But… "If I hurt you—"

Liam smiled so wide it felt like the sun had come back out. "Unless you're going to punch me directly in the ribs, you're not going to hurt me."

My face flushed. He tucked one hand behind my neck, pulling me in to kiss me. My hands moved of their own accord, gently sliding back up to his shoulders. The *heat* of his skin was so much more without clothing separating us. Last night when we'd been together in the same bed, it was all warmth. This put it to shame.

I pulled back and looked at my hands on his shoulders. Why was it so different without fabric between us? It shouldn't make that much of a difference, but it did. I moved my hands, tracing along the line of his collarbone and down the slope of his shoulders before coming back lower.

His body seemed bigger like this, where he sat so we were the same height. But touching him wasn't scary. New. Different. Not frightening.

Liam lifted my hand and kissed my palm, like he was testing my reaction to his mouth on my skin. I had imagined this. In the dark moments when I was feeling brave, while I was alone in my own bedroom. I tried to give myself the pleasure others talked about, with limited success.

There was also the time I'd found enough determination to look up some things on the internet. The determination didn't last long.

Hands slid along my hips, Liam's fingers teasing beneath the hem of my shirt. "Can I take this off?"

Biting my lip, I nodded.

He helped me pull it over my head and grinned as he tossed it aside. Liam's eyes roved over my skin, and there was no more doubt in my mind he wanted me. The heat of his skin was nothing compared to the heat in his gaze. And that single glance made me feel more than anything I'd ever tried to explore alone.

Liam pushed back for a second and kicked off his shoes. "Trust me, it's better when you don't have to stop for the shoes."

A laugh burst out of me, breaking the sexy tension strung between us. A good reminder that this didn't need to be fraught with emotion and the overbearing awareness that it was my first time. We could simply be ourselves. And as serious as Liam was, he was still the jokester too.

I followed his example and kicked off my shoes and socks, turning to place them by my suitcase. Arms came around me, and Liam held me to him, skin on skin. He kissed the tattoo at the top of my spine. "That you trust me enough to be your first is an honor, Mara. No matter if we have to stop or slow down. It's everything. I'm never going to forget it."

While I wasn't facing him, I felt braver, and I reached up to pull the straps of my bra off my shoulders. He softly kissed the skin where they had been, and I lost all of my breath. Finally, I *truly* understood what people meant when they said they had butterflies in their stomach.

Everything was stronger and more sensitive. One single touch of his lips on my skin and I had goose bumps everywhere.

I reached between us, getting my bra off and letting it fall to the floor. Liam skimmed his hands over my ribs and across my stomach. Every moment was the most I'd ever been touched. I felt drunk on the sensation, and we'd barely started.

Leaning back against him, I gave him my weight. Liam never ceased to amaze me in the way he understood my silence. He lifted me off the floor and took me to the bed, stretching us both out on top of the covers and holding me tight to his chest. I was exposed, and yet I didn't feel it.

"I promise I won't talk you to death," he said with a smile, stroking his hand down my spine. "But I have a couple more things to ask."

My fingers tapped twice lightly on his arm.

"You said 'show me.' What am I showing you tonight?"

I tilted my head to the side and met his gaze. He understood the question.

"Sex is more than just sex. And I would be happy to show you all of it. But I don't want to overdo it either."

He was holding me the way he had before. So familiar I could nearly forget we were half naked.

Nearly.

"What do you want to show me?" I asked softly.

"*Fuck*, Mara." Liam moved, rolling me beneath him. "I want to show you everything. Absolutely everything." He pressed a kiss to the corner of my mouth. "But tonight, if you'll let me, I want to show you what it's like to have someone touch you. Help you find pleasure, to help make it easier for you. And after that…"

"Yes," I whispered. Nothing he said scared me. I only wanted all of it with him.

Liam kissed me, holding back. He was always holding back, though he would never admit it. As much as I needed him to, I wanted to be in a place where he didn't have to, and this was the first step.

Removing his weight and sitting up beside me, he looked at me for the first time. My need to hide was instinctual, but I resisted. A flush rose beneath my skin, and he touched me. Softly at first, just brushing his fingers over my stomach and shoulders.

But it wasn't enough, and we both knew it.

I reached for him and pulled his face down to mine. My heart pounded in my ears. "Liam," I breathed his name, swallowing the need to stay quiet. This was *Liam*. "I'm a virgin, not broken. You don't need to be so careful with me."

He blew out a breath, shifting his weight over me once more, straddling my hips. The way his body pressed me down was comforting—like a living weighted blanket. I laughed, not imagining Liam would enjoy the comparison. He didn't ask, just smiled. "If you need to stop, tap me and keep tapping."

That I could do.

Every ounce of tension between us evaporated, and Liam dropped his mouth to my skin. Underneath my jaw and down my neck to the hollow of my throat. Gentle kisses across my skin. I never knew places like that could feel so good.

"I—" For once in my life, my voice was pressing against my lips, trying to break free, and I had no idea what to say.

Liam touched my breasts, covering them with his hands. My body responded like it had a mind of its own, arching and leaning into the touch. I was already feeling so much, all the sensations new and trying to draw my attention. But I *liked* it.

Lips pressed just below my neck—a kiss brushing and moving downward. Until his mouth was directly between my breasts, and somehow it wasn't strange.

"I want to learn everything you like," he whispered into my skin. "What makes your breath catch and what makes you moan."

He closed his mouth over my nipple, and he got his wish. I gasped, my nipple hardening under his tongue and how it moved. Liam smiled despite the way he was kissing my skin.

It felt incredible. I ran my hands over the buzz of his

hair, holding him to me because I didn't want him to stop. Ever.

"Just like that," he said, lifting his eyes to mine and running a finger over the taut skin. Flickers and sparks flowed from his touch downward before he sealed his mouth over my other nipple and repeated the process.

He never stopped moving his hands either, sliding them over my ribs and up over my shoulders. Liam was drowning me in touch, and at the moment, I was regretting all the time I'd spent without it.

Lower. His mouth moved lower, leaving a trail of fluttering kisses over my stomach. My nipples tightened further in the absence of his mouth, the coolness of air on wet skin. And my heart definitely, *definitely* skipped a beat, because he was at the waistband of my jeans.

One look up at me to make sure I was still with him, and he undid my belt. He was right—I was glad we'd ditched our shoes before all this started. I did not have the patience to wait for him to do it now. I was barely breathing, eager for him to strip the rest of my clothes off me.

Liam kissed my hip bones as he peeled my jeans off me. Every part of my body was alert and aware. There was no hesitation in Liam's movements or touch now.

I made the last move. It felt important to be the one to slip my fingers into my underwear and push them down. Liam met me halfway, catching my hands and taking over at my knees.

I was naked with him. Liam looked at me like I was everything he wanted in the world, and I always wanted *that* look.

"You're incredible," he whispered.

I shook my head.

Liam only smiled before skimming his hands up my

thighs and parting my legs. Adrenaline slammed through me so quickly, I was shaking. Everyone talked about this. The women at the ranch talked about their men. They weren't shy about sharing, and I always wondered what it would be like.

Tugging me down to the end of the bed, Liam sank to his knees. The smirk on his face did strange things to my insides. And his maintaining eye contact as he leaned in sent heat spiraling through my core. I *wanted,* and I didn't even know how to want.

Liam put his mouth on me.

Right between my legs.

"Oh—" The sound slipped out of me. It was strange and new, and *why* did that feel so good?

He gripped my thighs with his fingers and pushed me open farther, licking into me. The sound he made was that of a starved man. I'd never known how much I needed to hear it. My arms shook, and I gave in, lying back on the bed and surrendering to the feeling of him.

I couldn't breathe. Couldn't move. All I could do was feel Liam's lips and tongue. The way he scooped his hands under my thighs and tightened his grip in order to consume me.

Nameless pleasure rose under my skin, leading to something. The only orgasms I'd ever had were desperate and quick, driven by physical need and nothing else. This was so much more.

Dizziness whirled through me. He was taking his time. No urgency in the movements of Liam's mouth. Only slow, luxurious enjoyment, and no sign of him ever wanting to stop or move on.

I fell into a place of only pleasure. A simple existence of enjoyment and newness. Delicious, honeyed fire drifting along my skin. But I wasn't growing closer to anything, and a small ball of anxiety grew in my chest.

Liam sealed his mouth over me and sucked, long and slow, before he released me and crawled onto the bed, lining his body up with mine. "What happened?"

I raised my eyebrows in question, and he smiled. His mouth shone with *me*. My stomach swooped at the sight.

"You tensed up," he said. "Your whole body went tight as a bowstring."

"I—" Swallowing, I tried to find the words. "I wasn't… I don't think I can. I loved it—"

"Sex isn't only about orgasms." He smiled and laughed softly. "They're great. But it's more than that. I want to show you pleasure. As long as it feels good, the rest will come."

I breathed out and wrapped my arms around his neck. "It felt good," I whispered. "So good. I just—"

Liam's hand slipped between my legs and grazed the most sensitive part of me. I gasped. Gentle circles around it that brought forward more of the delicious, addictive feeling from under his tongue.

"Orgasms are learned," Liam whispered in my ear. "It takes time to figure out what you like, what you *love*, and what makes you scream."

Screaming was out of the question. I could barely make a sound voluntarily. Being able to scream? I shuddered. *Yes.* That sounded amazing. Being able to scream and not worry about how loud I was or what might happen? That would mean I was healing.

The small circles grew faster. One spot he touched made my hips arch into his hand, and he noticed, going back there and teasing it. The feeling built under his single finger, everything tightening and making me shake.

"Liam." I sounded strangled and frantic, my fingers clinging to his shoulders. It was there—so close. Right behind my eyes.

"I've got you," he said. "I've got you."

His voice reached inside me and lit the fuse. One single burst of pleasure blowing outward in a nova before disappearing. I shook, my body feeling as weak as if I'd just run a mile.

"Are you all right?"

I yanked him down to me and kissed him. Yes. Yes, I was all right. Yes, I wanted him. Yes, I wanted more. I loved not being afraid. I loved the freedom I was feeling right now, and I never wanted to let it go. "More."

He kissed me back for one more long moment. "Stay right here."

Liam stood up from the bed, and I watched him unbuckle his jeans and let them fall to the floor. It was already clear even before his underwear hit the floor how aroused he was. For me.

And oh—

He was turned away, opening the drawer of his dresser. Seeing him naked stole my breath. The strong lines of his shoulders ran down his back. Pure strength resided in his thighs, and the rest of the view showed me exactly why he filled out his jeans so well.

Then he turned around.

The condom was already on, and it didn't make him any less impressive. This was the moment I couldn't turn back from, and I didn't want to.

Liam came back and lifted me, guiding us back to the top of the bed where there were pillows and softness. He kissed me gently. "I'm sorry this might hurt."

Parting my thighs once more, I *felt* him. Already, it was bigger than I'd imagined it feeling. My body still rang with the echoes of pleasure, and I found it easier to relax.

He distracted me, kissing me deeply as he eased in. And in. And in. It hurt, and it didn't. I couldn't breathe with the feeling of fullness, and I ached, still wanting more.

"There," Liam whispered against my lips. "We're there."

All I could do was hold on to him and say again the only word I could think of. "More."

Chapter 16

Liam

I'D NEVER SEEN anything more beautiful than Mara underneath me, finding pleasure beneath my mouth and hands. Now I was inside her and…

It was everything.

Pain warred with pleasure on Mara's face. "More," she whispered.

I meant what I said to her. It was an honor to be with her like this. My entire life could pass, and nothing would compare to her trust in me.

Everything in me wanted more of this. I wasn't going to last long at all. Her body hugged mine like it was meant to be there. I could barely see straight.

Gently, I rocked into her, savoring Mara's tiny gasp. She squeezed down on me, and I went blind. "Mara." My voice was ragged. "You feel… God, you feel so good," I told her.

She lifted her hips toward mine. A silent invitation to continue. I couldn't take her the way I wanted to tonight—

whatever she needed, though, I would give her. But she was surprising the hell out of me. Inside my Mara was a woman who wanted more than life had allowed her, and despite her nerves, she was working to take it.

I wanted everything with her. Every first and every experience. The raw, male part of me loved that I was her first. Beyond her trust and what it meant for her to trust me, I *wanted* to be the only one who touched her. I wanted Mara to learn everything with me so we could grow together. There was no comparison to learning someone's pleasure. Already, I saw the way she responded to rhythm and pressure. When her body was ready, my woman would love hard and fast.

So would I.

She gripped my shoulders and rocked upward, her whole body shuddering, her expression somewhere between delirious and pure determination.

I moved. A slow, easy rhythm for us both. A beginning. No matter the rhythm, I'd wanted her too long. Minutes were all I had. They were going to be the best minutes I could give her.

Rolling, smooth movements that brushed against her body. That small orgasm from my fingers was a victory I wanted to use. I made sure every time I moved, she felt it again. And again. And again. Exactly the same speed I'd used with my fingers.

A low moan sent the rest of the blood I had south. Mara's voice already turned me on outside of the bedroom. Hearing it like this? Undone and out of pure need?

I wanted to record the way she sounded so I could listen to it over and over again. Her voice was a craving I needed to satisfy, and as if she knew, another low moan reached my ears.

Exactly what I needed.

"Fuck." The word slipped out of me, all my control

gone. Lightning blazed down my spine, unleashing pleasure and heat. Three more thrusts, and I came, her name on my lips.

My soul left my body and my vision disappeared while the waves hit me, the orgasm slicing through me so sharply I went rigid. I braced myself over Mara, trying to make sure I didn't crush her or hurt her while my body stole all my control.

I heaved in a breath and looked down at her, forcing myself back into my body. Mara's eyes locked on mine, and she smiled. "It might be cliché," I said, breathless, "but I usually last longer."

She laughed, eyes sparkling. Words were building in her eyes. "I…if there's no pressure for me, there's no pressure for you."

As I rocked my hips again, her spine arched. A good sign. "Did I hurt you?"

Mara shook her head. I noticed the way she was touching me, her hands on my arms and chest. She needed more than this, and I needed to hold her. "I need to take care of the condom," I said. "I'll be right back."

She winced as I pulled out of her. I might not have hurt her, but it didn't mean she wouldn't be sore. With the condom gone, I cleaned myself up as quickly as I could, grabbing a warm washcloth for Mara and pulling on a pair of underwear.

"Here," I said. "Let me."

"What?" Mara caught my wrist and scrambled upright. "You don't have to do that."

I watched her face, trying to filter through her panic to figure out what was bothering her. "Are you sure?"

Her cheeks turned pink, and she looked down. Whatever the reaction was, it was a long-buried instinct. "I'm happy to take care of you, Mara, but I would never force you."

Taking the washcloth out of my hand, she slipped into the bathroom for a few minutes. While she was in the bathroom, I stripped back the comforter and made sure we had a different blanket.

I heard the toilet flush, and Mara came back out of the bathroom, still more tense than she had been. I held out my arms, and relief spilled over when she stepped into them without hesitation.

I arranged us in the bed, savoring the softness of her curves and the warmth of her skin and making sure we were cozied under the blankets before leaning over her. Brushing the hair out of her face, I kissed her forehead. "Did I overstep, sweetheart?"

She shook her head, forehead still pressed against my lips. "No."

The way she clung to me now, I never wanted to let her go. Her body melted as she relaxed, just like she had last night. "Are you all right?" I asked. "Are you bleeding?"

"No. I feel…good."

"But something upset you. It's okay to tell me."

Mara's hand fluttered on my arms. She was struggling with words. Part of me hoped it was because she was happy.

"We don't have to talk right now," I whispered. "I'm more than happy to hold you."

She curled into me and blew out a long, slow breath. It was easier for her to talk without looking at me. I loved seeing her face, but I understood the tightrope of vulnerability she was walking. She might struggle with it for the rest of her life, and if she did, I would still be with her. I could encourage her toward healing, but there was only so much one mind could take.

"I don't…want you to think it was you," she said softly. "I want this. I want you. And more."

I stroked my hand down her side, waiting for more words.

"You already did so much," she finally said. "You did everything."

Suddenly, I understood. In all the time she spent with The Family, the men did nothing. On top of everything new, letting me take care of her in the aftermath pressed that boundary.

"I like taking care of you, Mara. Whatever form it takes. Especially if it brings you pleasure."

Her mouth was pressed against my chest, and I felt the way she bit her lip. "It did."

We held each other in silence for a few minutes. It was still relatively early in the evening, but I didn't see us leaving this bed. We'd had one hell of a day.

"Was I okay?" Mara whispered.

"Were you okay?" It hit me she was asking about sex. There was a reason I put on underwear—to lessen the temptation of having her again and again. Because I'd only had one taste, and as far as I was concerned, it would never be enough. "The only reason I'm not naked with you right now is because you're a temptation I don't think I can resist. I want you so much it hurts to breathe. Watching you—*tasting* you—god, Mara. I don't have the words."

She pulled her head back to look at me, her eyes filled with hope. "Really?"

"If I made you feel anything different, I've been an absolutely shitty boyfriend. I don't want to hurt you. Otherwise, you might have to witness me begging."

I liked the spark that appeared in her eyes, followed by a smile. "I might like that."

I covered her mouth with mine, pressing her deeper into the mattress. "Yeah?"

She gave a nod, along with a smile.

"How do you really feel?" I asked. "Physically."

She thought about it, and Mara wiggling her hips back and forth did nothing for the state of my body, already so hard again I ached.

"I'm a little sore. There's a twinge inside I'm not used to. But not nearly as bad as I expected."

That brought a laugh out of me. "Good. And if I were to do this?" I slid my hand down her side again, slipping between her legs to find her clit. Not inside her—just teasing.

"Oh," she gasped, biting her lip. Her body betrayed her, pushing back against my palm.

"Too much?"

"No." She dug one hand into my shoulder.

I couldn't keep the smile off my face as she closed her eyes, and I focused on bringing her over the edge of pleasure again.

Chapter 17

Mara

THE HOT WATER flowed over both of us in Liam's shower. I'd thought his bedroom was incredible, but the bathroom was amazing too. His shower was the size of my entire bathroom.

At the moment, I couldn't see it, because Liam had my back pressed into the subway tile wall, and he was on his knees. His strength and his lips were really the only things keeping me upright, given the way my knees were weak.

Last night, he'd teased me until I came again, and every time I did, it felt easier. Liam found the little movements that made all the difference, like the way his tongue curled under my clit and made my body clench and shudder with anticipation and pleasure.

We woke up in the middle of the night, and he rolled me onto my knees and used his mouth again from behind. I saw stars and moaned into the pillows, falling asleep almost immediately in the aftermath.

I no longer had any doubt. Liam didn't care about my lack of experience—he was creating my experience. He shut down the part of my mind shouting at me to feel guilty for taking, and he gave without reservation.

When he sank to his knees in the shower, my jaw dropped. But the feeling of his mouth wasn't one I could resist. Not now that I knew what it felt like.

Pleasure broke over me like the flowing water, and I heard my own voice echo off the walls. Liam didn't stop until I was braced on his shoulders, barely able to stand.

"I'm never going to get tired of that," he said. "Or that sound."

I pressed my lips together.

"Does that embarrass you?" His tone was teasing.

"A little," I admitted. "It's not a compliment you think about."

He pressed me back into the wall once more. "It is for me. I'll tell you as many times as you need to hear it. You're beautiful. I'm completely addicted to the sound of your voice, and—"

He broke off and kissed me. Whatever was meant to be at the end of his sentence made my heart pound. He couldn't have meant that, right?

Liam sighed. "I don't want to leave this shower. But I want to check in at the ranch to see if they found anything."

I nodded. "I should get to work. I'm behind."

"Daniel's made it clear. We're both covered until this is all figured out. You can do whatever you like. But…"

"But?"

"Would you hate me if I said I would prefer you weren't alone?"

I froze, fear suddenly running down my spine. "Do you think they'll come here? Is the ranch not safe?"

"The ranch *is* safe," Liam said. "It is. And I don't know if there's danger. That's what makes me nervous."

Smiling, I grabbed some shampoo and washed my hair. Someone worrying about me like that shouldn't make me smile, but it did. "You're sure Daniel is fine with it?"

"Yes." His tone held no room for argument.

I blew out a breath. Until he mentioned it, I hadn't noticed. Not being alone eased my nerves. "I can hang out at Deja Brew," I said. "Or I can come with you. I can even stay here. Unless you don't want me here alone."

Liam chuckled. "I have nothing to hide, and I don't care. It might be a while, though. You sure you want to be here by yourself?"

No. I didn't actually want that. "Take me to Lena's, please."

"Will do."

Showering with him, drying off with him, and getting dressed with him felt domestic in a way I didn't dare to love. It was so easy to love things that could get taken away in a heartbeat.

I stopped.

That was a thought I needed to address. I shouldn't sabotage something before it started.

Liam helped me into the truck, and his hands felt different on me now. Brand-new awareness of every touch, because he'd been *inside* me now. I'd come for him, and he'd seen all of me.

I wanted to pull him back into the house and not let him go. Now, my mind was open to the possibilities, and I wanted to explore them. But we both needed to know if Jude had found anything, and I needed a mental break. Daniel was gracious in letting me off the hook for work. This once, I would take advantage.

"I'm sorry people know about us before you were ready," Liam said.

I slid across the seat of his truck and leaned against him. His arm came around my waist, holding me in place. We were driving slowly through town, or I already knew he would ask me to buckle up again. But Deja Brew was only a few blocks away now.

"They were always going to know."

"Still doesn't mean you were ready for it."

Smiling, I turned my face into his shoulder. "Once Lena and Evie see me getting out of your truck, it's all over."

"Selfishly, I'm glad. Because I don't know if I could leave without kissing you."

"Good."

He squeezed my hip. "I was thinking about something. Kind of along the same lines, but I wanted to ask you first."

I put my hand over his and tapped twice.

"All this time, I've been nervous about letting people see my home. I'm not sure whether it was self-preservation or worry about not living up to who they think I am. But your reaction made me realize I've been hiding."

Another two taps. "I love your house."

"I thought I'd ask the guys if we could have family dinner at my house. It could be a lot. Especially if people know about us. Which is why I'm asking you first."

We pulled over in front of Deja Brew, and he turned off the truck. It was nerve-racking to know we would be watched at a get-together like that. But we would be watched anyway, no matter if we were at the ranch or Liam's house. "You don't need my permission," I said quietly.

"No, but I want it. Because I want you to stay, Mara. I'm not ready to let you go yet."

I hid my smile in the sleeve of his shirt, because I hoped he'd say exactly that. Thinking about going back to my house alone like I had all these years? It no longer held any appeal. My little cabin was my sanctuary, and I loved it. But it was also lonely. "Yes, please. To both."

Liam opened the truck door and jumped to the ground before turning and lifting me out then kissing me.

Hard.

By the time we came up for air, we were tangled together, and I'd completely forgotten we were in public. He held me tight, and I closed my eyes. I'd never felt safer than when I was with him. "I'll be back as soon as I can."

Two taps.

"Have fun with them."

"I'll try."

Liam watched me until I got inside before he started the truck and left.

"Well." Lena's voice came from behind me. "I guess I know what kinds of texts had you smiling the other day."

I turned, not even trying to hide my smile. She was already moving and making me a drink. "We tried to keep it quiet. Didn't work. I thought you might already know."

Evie stuck her head out of the kitchen and grinned. "We kind of guessed after the wedding, but we know better than to jump to conclusions now."

"Can I hang out for a while? Neither of us wants me to be alone."

Lena stared at me. "Girl, you can stay as long as you want! You know that. And I think that might be the most words I've heard you say at one time."

Spending time with Liam seemed to have that effect on me. My words didn't seem nearly out of reach today.

"You guys went somewhere?" Lena asked. "I tried getting Jude to spill the details, but he wouldn't. And made it very clear I wasn't allowed to ask him again."

Evie snickered, and Lena blushed. I'd heard enough

about Jude and Lena's relationship to know what it meant. The way they exchanged power made sense for them. It wasn't something I wanted, but it made both of them happy.

"So, you and Liam…" Lena cleared her throat and handed me my drink.

"We went to Phoenix. It…didn't go well. We might have to go back. But the two of us are very good."

Lena looked at me carefully. "Is it something you want to talk about?"

Sighing, I shook my head. "Not today."

"Okay." She grinned. "I'll only grill you about Liam, then. He dropped you off. Does that mean you stayed over?"

I backed over to the couches and chairs. "Maybe."

"Oh my god, I need all the details."

Evie took off her apron. "Only if Mara wants to give them." The way she glanced at me… I recognized it. They might not know what I'd been through, but survivors of trauma could recognize each other. Everyone knew *something* had happened, but Evie and I always understood more.

"There's not much to tell," I admitted. "We've both…liked each other for a while. At the wedding, he helped me when I had a panic attack, and not long after, we decided to try. The texts that made me smile were him asking me on a date."

Evie pulled me into a hug. "Girl, I love it when you talk."

"Thank you."

"If this is because of Liam, it's a good thing."

I nodded. "It is. A little. And I'm tired of letting it control me. It's not easy." The last words came out softer.

"No," she agreed. "It's not."

The door chimed, and a woman I now recognized entered. Brynn. Evie and Lena both waved hello. Her face lit up when she saw me. "I didn't run into you this time."

"No."

"How are you?" Lena asked.

Brynn kept smiling, but it was tight. "I'm good. Don't have too much time before I have to be over to the Mission Club. Waitressing." She shrugged. "It works, for now."

"Hmm." Evie made the sound low enough for only me to hear. "That could be interesting."

I raised my eyebrows.

"I can't be here all the time anymore," she said. "And as much as Lena says it's fine, it's not. There's too much to do by herself, and she's really behind. Brynn has been coming in for a few weeks, and she seems really nice. There's something familiar about her."

We shared a look. I hadn't interacted with her enough to know, but I trusted Evie's judgment. Maybe Brynn was running from something, just like we both had. If she was, Deja Brew was the perfect place for her to be.

"I'll be right back," she said. "Lena, come here for a second."

They stepped into the kitchen together, leaving Brynn and me alone. They both liked her. Talking to friends was easy. Strangers, not so much. But if she might work here, she'd be part of our world soon enough.

I swallowed. "I'm sorry. The last couple of times, I was…preoccupied."

"Oh, it was totally my fault. I *literally* ran into you. I swear I'm not usually that clumsy."

The silence was awkward for a couple of seconds. I hadn't talked to someone new in a long time. "You just moved here?"

"Yeah. Seemed like a nice change of pace. It's good." Her tone was too cheery for her to be telling the truth. "So far, at least."

"It's a good place to be."

Lena came out of the kitchen with her usual burst of energy. "Sorry about that. Brynn, I have a question for you."

"Shoot."

"Do you like working at the Mission Club?"

The woman laughed. "It's a job, and not the worst one I've had. But not really."

"Well." Lena put her hands on her hips. "Evie here can't work full time anymore, and I need help. Would you be willing to come in for an interview?"

Brynn's mouth dropped open. "Really?"

"If you like coffee and baking more than being a waitress," Evie said.

"Yes. Absolutely."

"Later this week? I'm swamped for the next couple of days. But swing by when you're free."

The look on Brynn's face made the three of us smile. "Yes. Absolutely. I will. *Thank you*! I'm so sorry I have to go right now."

"Don't be late," Lena said. "We'll see you later."

She grabbed her coffee and paused, like she was going to say something else. But she simply smiled and waved before speed-walking out the door.

"I think she'll fit in," Evie said. "And at the very least, if she doesn't work out, she'll have something more on her résumé than the Mission Club."

I'd never been. It was an older bar on the outskirts of town and catered to a similar clientele. It didn't have a reputation for being a friendly place to anyone who wasn't a man over fifty. Working there as a woman was likely far worse than she let on.

"We'll give it a go," Lena said. "It worked out well the last time I took in a stray."

Evie rolled her eyes, but she smiled too. "You going to be okay this afternoon?"

"I can help while I'm here," I said.

"You already work too hard, Mara."

I slipped past Lena into the kitchen before she could stop me, and I grabbed an apron. "You can pay me in cookies and coffee. Besides, I don't know how long I'm going to be here. When Liam comes back—"

"Sold," Lena said. "Because I have some *questions* for that man. At this point, he's almost as bad as Jude with all the waiting."

"I've got to go. Mara, I'll see you at family dinner," Evie called on her way out the door.

"Bye." I hoped she heard me. Words were easier today, but raising my voice was not.

"All right. We're making chocolate chip." Lena pointed to the stool at the worktable, and I sat. "Roll the balls and put them onto the trays, and you'll be my favorite forever."

"I thought I was already your favorite?"

"Oh, absolutely. And you'll be even more my favorite once you tell me about this date you went on."

I made the motion to zip my lips.

"Come on," she begged, bouncing on her toes. "I'm dying here. Just a bit."

Taking a long sip of my drink, I made her wait. Being on this side of the story was fun. "We went paragliding."

"You *what*?"

I started rolling the balls of cookie dough. "You said a bit."

Out front, the door chimed, and Lena pinned me with a stare. "I'm not done with this. When I get back, I'll get it out of you."

She went to help the customer, and all I did was smile.

Chapter 18

Liam

EVERYONE GATHERED in the lodge except Grant, still on his honeymoon in Ireland with Cori. Usually, I would make some sort of joke about being the last one to the party, but I didn't feel like joking. This was serious. I knew exactly where Mara was, and I still felt a low-grade panic in my gut.

I sat heavily in one of the chairs. "If this is the way all of you felt, I owe every one of you an apology."

Chuckles came from all around.

"No, you don't," Lucas said. "It's not something you can understand until you're in the middle of it."

"You're telling me." I scrubbed a hand over my face, which drew attention to my bandage.

Daniel leaned forward on the table. "You should get checked out by Dr. Gold."

"I'm fine."

"I know you are, but you should get looked at, regardless."

I rolled my eyes. "They got a few hits on me. I've taken worse beatings from the people in this room."

Noah smirked. More than one of those beatings had been from him when we'd both needed to get out some aggression. "You need to get looked at in case they find the guys who jumped you. Get the injuries documented."

"I can, but they're not going to find them. Let's be honest. They're not going to look."

"Probably not," Harlan shrugged. "Do it all the same. Just in case."

"Fine." I sighed.

Jude crossed his arms and settled deeper into his chair. "Tell us again, and the rest of it. So they can hear it too. And you're not under time pressure."

I recounted everything from the trip, including everything that happened in the courtroom and from the attack. The things that happened between Mara and me? Those were only for us.

When I finished, I looked around the table. "I know it hasn't been long. Is there anything?"

Daniel shook his head. "Not really. Reached out through contacts, and the Phoenix Police Department is treating it as a random act of violence. Nothing was stolen from you, and you live out of state with minor injuries. We'll be lucky if they even follow up."

"They *did* look for camera footage," Jude said. "There wasn't any. The alley is in a blind spot, which is either the luckiest break of all time or premeditation."

"Or a spot where they regularly grab people."

"I'd like to think if it was a spot with regularly occurring crime, they'd take steps to correct the blind spot," Noah said. "But you never know."

I leaned my elbows on my knees. "It wasn't random. Nothing about it *felt* random. They weren't going for my wallet. They were going for *me*. I could be making it up, but I don't think so. I wish I could explain the way they looked at me in the courtroom."

Daniel held up a hand. "We believe you, and I agree. There are too many coincidences."

"What do you think they want?" Harlan asked me. "Targeting Mara, I understand. It's fucked up and rage-inducing, but I can see the motivation. But why you?"

My mouth flattened into a line. Mara being chosen as a child bride to be raped at will by all the men of The Family wasn't my story to share. Daniel and Jude didn't even know that particular piece. "It isn't mine to tell," I said roughly. "But suffice it to say, he wants her alone, scared, and isolated. I don't know what reaction they would have had if a woman had been with her. But to them? I'm a threat."

"Noted," Jude said with a nod. "We're on alert. I have a few programs running for any mention of your names, The Family, and some other conditional results. And you know how we work. Keep us apprised of where you and Mara are for now, so we can be on guard."

I blew out a breath. "She's staying with me for the time being. Not that we feel like her house or the ranch aren't secure. We both feel better not being alone."

They all grinned, and I pretended not to notice.

"How's it going?" Noah asked. "Seriously."

"Seriously…it's going well. I'm happy I took the risk, especially now." I looked around at each of them. "And I appreciate you holding back on all the jokes. After some of the shit I gave you guys, I deserve it."

"You do," Jude said with a smirk. "But we really are happy for you. And I think I speak for all of us when I say we understand why jokes aren't welcome right now."

"I don't promise shit after this is resolved, though," Harlan said.

A laugh slipped out of me. "I know I've got it coming. When is Grant back?"

"They're coming in tomorrow," Daniel said. "They'll be around for family dinner."

Family dinner...

Resting Warrior was so different now from when we'd started this as seven broken men trying to do some good in the world. With Grant and Cori back from their honeymoon, baby Avery, along with Emma pregnant, family dinners actually *felt* like family.

Asking Mara about hosting it at my house had been more nerve-racking than I was willing to admit. I didn't doubt my place in this family. Every man in this room was strong, loyal, and steadfast. I was honored to be here at all.

I did my best to push down the feelings of self-doubt and the deeper sense of worthlessness that popped up in moments like these. Today, they weren't staying where I wanted them, and they filled me, wanting attention.

If I was here with these men and they called me one of their own, why was my whole life riddled with people who had abandoned me? And deeper was the worry that Mara would figure out whatever those people had seen and leave me too.

An image painted itself in my head—coming home here in Garnet Bend and finding Mara gone. Nothing more than a note. Like Jenny had. The hollowness in my chest—

I wouldn't recover from that again. Not with Mara.

All those thoughts weren't real, and this family wasn't about to turn its back on me. I needed to reach out and take the plunge the same way I finally had with Mara. Fear was never a good motivation.

"About family dinner." They all looked at me. "Would you mind if I hosted it at my house?"

Stunned silence fell around the table.

"I know it's always here. I'm trying something new, and aside from Daniel, none of you have ever been to my house."

Jude chuckled. "I'm all for that. Lena will lose her shit."

"Evie too," Lucas said. "Are you prepared for that?"

Spreading my hands wide, I shook my head. "I have absolutely no idea."

Daniel watched me, and I met his gaze. "You don't have to prove anything to us, Liam."

"I know. It's something I want to do."

"Then your place it is."

Noah looked at me. "Does this mean you're cooking?"

"Scared?"

He stood and clapped me on the shoulder. "I'll let you know after I taste it. Gotta get over to the barn."

"Is there anything else you need from me?" I asked them. "I know you said I'm covered."

"And we meant it," Harlan said.

Daniel stood too. "Just keep us posted about what happens as far as the lawyers go. We all know there's plenty he can do from prison, but he's still limited. If he's out, it changes the ball game." Then he smiled. "Go spend time with her. It's where you want to be, and more than anything, we need you to be where your focus is."

"Take care of her, and cook us a good meal. But first, get checked out at the hospital," Lucas added.

"Thanks."

All I wanted was to get back to Mara. But I didn't want her to sit with me in the hospital for no reason when she could be relaxing with Lena.

The whole thing took longer than I wanted and was exactly what I expected. Surface-level injuries with instructions to get some rest. But my injuries were officially documented. Even if they found The Family members who jumped me, proof didn't exist, and my injuries weren't severe enough to get them jail time.

I texted Daniel, confirming being checked out, and headed back to Deja Brew. As soon as my mind knew I was heading toward Mara, the whole world got brighter.

The bell over Deja Brew's door rang as I pushed inside, and laughter spilled out of the kitchen. Both Mara's and Lena's laughter. Her laugh was the best sound in the world. Light and life and sweetness all wrapped up into one.

"You're here to steal her from me, aren't you?" Lena peeked out of the kitchen and made a face. "Mara is a very good assistant. I'm not sure you can have her back."

"That's too bad. I was looking forward to her company."

Lena winked. "I'm just kidding. Come on back. She's elbows-deep in cookie dough and frosting. We'll need a minute."

I followed her back to the kitchen and froze in the doorway. Mara sat on a stool with the biggest smile on her face. Purple frosting painted her hands and arms. A smudge also graced her forehead.

With a frosting bag, she painted purple swirls on pale sugar cookies, and I couldn't stop looking at her. She was luminous. No worry weighed down her shoulders.

This was who Mara was when assholes like Malcolm weren't making her question her worth. Or pushing her to think she had no one in her corner. She was vibrant and beautiful, and rage burned in me at the men who'd robbed her of a life full of joy.

Her smile didn't falter when she saw me. She held out a cookie, eyes sparkling. I rounded the table and took a bite. *Fuck*, no one made cookies like Lena. "That's incredible."

"Mara did most of the work."

Mara shook her head and rolled her eyes, still smiling. "No."

"Do you want to stay? You're having fun."

She glanced at Lena, who'd stepped out to the front of the shop. "I can have fun with you, too."

"I was hoping you'd say that. And if you want, you can help me plan for family dinner."

"They said yes?"

"They did."

Lena was back and pulling off her apron. "Said yes to what?"

"A surprise."

She narrowed her eyes at me. "I hate surprises."

Mara and I laughed. "It's a good thing, I promise. Jude will tell you, I'm sure."

"I need to wash my hands."

I lifted Mara off the stool, simply happy to have her in my arms again. Her cheeks turned pink, and I was looking forward to turning her that color as soon as we got back to my house. More than once.

As soon as the bathroom door closed, Lena turned on me. "This is the part where I tell you I'll kick your ass if you hurt her."

I slipped my hands into the pockets of my jeans. "Unfortunately, you're at the back of the line."

"I'm sure Jude can slip me to the front to get a few punches in."

I grinned. "I'd like to see it. But I won't, because the last thing I want for Mara is pain. I—"

Mara came back from the bathroom, and I swallowed the words that had been about to slip out so easily. It wasn't time yet.

Lena still looked at me, but she nodded, accepting my words. I would never begrudge people protecting her, even from me.

"Ready."

We waved goodbye to Lena, and I pulled Mara into me before I lifted her into the truck again. There was only so long I could live without her lips. "I missed you."

She lifted her chin in response, wordlessly asking for more. I gave everything I had, knowing I was about to jump off a cliff into love with this woman, and I wasn't afraid of the fall.

Chapter 19

Mara

MY HEART SAT in my throat. Nerves jangled in my gut, restless energy making me want to pace. Instead, I turned around Liam's living room one more time and made sure everything was perfect. If I was nervous, Liam was at least three times worse.

I didn't *want* either of us to be nervous. This was our family. They weren't going to walk into this house and judge it the way Liam was afraid of, but it was still daunting. We were together. Hosting family dinner *together*. The night in front of us held weight.

Hopefully, everyone would have some nerves in this situation.

After a lazy day yesterday, Liam and I spent time in bed. And on his couch. And then back in bed again, we finally went to the grocery store to get everything we needed for family dinner.

We made lasagna and nearly burned it because we got

distracted by each other. Liam unlocked needs in my body I'd ignored my entire life, and now I couldn't get enough. I was sore and didn't care. All I wanted was him.

Clinking glass drew my attention from the dining room. Liam was setting out glasses, entirely focused. At the moment, he was like me. The silent one. Quiet. His nerves made him retreat.

I wrapped my arms around him from behind. He stopped what he was doing and breathed with me. I *felt* the breaths. I tapped his chest twice. It meant yes, but I hoped he knew what it was now.

It will be okay. I am here with you.

"I finished the salad. The garlic bread is in the oven."

Two taps.

Liam turned in my arms. Worry clung to every feature. "I'm nervous too," I whispered.

"I know I shouldn't be." He sighed. "Can't seem to shake it."

"They'll be here soon, and you'll see. They're going to love this place as much as I do."

I felt the breath catch in his chest at the word *love*. He'd come just as close to saying it—or similar—half a dozen times in the last two days.

"I hope so."

Car doors slammed outside. "You're about to find out."

Noah and Kate were the first, Lena and Jude pulling up right behind them. Noah looked at the outside of the house. "Man, this house is great. I had no idea you lived over here. Has this always been your house in Garnet Bend?"

"Not for the first couple of months I was here. But since then."

The two men shook hands in the way men did when they were already friends but were entering a new domain. They were on Liam's turf. It wasn't the only handshake we would see tonight.

Kate held a covered dish and smiled. "Hey."

I waved hello and took the dish from her hands. Round as it was, I suspected a pie. The women of the ranch had banded together once they'd found out we were doing dinner here. Drinks and dessert were coming with them. We would be overrun with treats.

Lena immediately pulled me into a hug. "If this was your idea, it was a good one."

"It wasn't, actually," I said.

"Well, it's still a good idea."

Out of the corner of my eye, I saw Jude and Liam shake hands as well. And suddenly there were so many people, I couldn't keep track of who I'd said hi to. Lucas, Evie, and baby Avery were here, along with Daniel and a very pregnant Emma. And Cori and Grant, freshly back from Ireland.

She glowed, and Grant did too, in his own way. They were back, but they barely took their eyes off each other. Grace and Harlan were last, but they were just as much in awe of the place as everyone else.

Liam's entire house was a mess of laughter and conversation. The guys teased him a little about how well decorated the place was, but there was no malice in it. Liam's shoulders were easy, and he relaxed into his element.

"Girl." Evie pulled Cori away from Grant. "We need to hear about Ireland. Because I *desperately* want to go."

"It's incredible. Everything is beautiful, and I want to go back." She flushed. "We didn't sight-see as much as we'd planned."

Evie laughed, drawing the rest of the women to us. Avery fussed a little, and I reached for her instinctually. With all the intensity and everything happening, I hadn't seen the baby in a couple of weeks. Every time I saw her, she was so much bigger.

Her pale blond hair was fluffy and soft. I brushed it off her forehead, and she reached up and caught my own hair. "Hi, baby," I whispered.

She smiled up at me.

"You're okay, Mara?" Evie asked.

I nodded without taking my eyes off Avery. I was more than okay. Calm and easy.

"Mara," Liam said, appearing at my side, laughing. "Of all the things we needed, we forgot ice. I'll go to the store to grab some."

He stopped, seeing me with Avery in my arms. His gaze flicked from me to the baby and back before he smiled. A strange contradiction of a smile. Joy, but at the same time, his eyes filled with heat, as if seeing me with Avery reminded him of all day yesterday.

And last night.

And hopefully later tonight.

"You look good with a baby in your arms," he said quietly.

I smiled, my voice not choosing to make itself known. But my stomach flipped. Liam leaned in and kissed my temple. "Thank you for everything."

"Liam," Noah called. "Let me go grab the ice, man."

"You sure?"

He held up his keys. "Yeah, I got it. We need you to make sure everything else is ready. It smells amazing."

"Thanks."

No one even blinked at the sight of Liam and me together. I hadn't thought they would, but it was nice to have the confirmation. Knowing something and feeling it were two completely different things.

Avery fussed again, and Evie sighed with a smile. "Let

me take her. She's probably getting hungry. I'll feed her real quick before we sit down."

I transferred Avery gently back into her mother's arms and sighed. Having kids around brought back how much I missed that aspect of The Family's compound.

Liam tucked his arms around me and pressed a kiss right above my ear. "Ready for dinner?"

I placed my hand over his and tapped twice.

In the dining room, Daniel helped Emma into a seat. "We'll probably have to go to Seattle," he said. "I know the FBI wanted the trial on the East Coast, but jurisdictionally, it's a nightmare."

Emma made a face. "I wish it would go faster. Now I'm not supposed to fly."

Daniel grinned and kissed his fiancée. "It won't take long."

She glared back. "I still don't like it."

For the first time, I truly understood her. After what she'd gone through, she didn't want to be apart from Daniel any more than I wanted to be apart from Liam. There was safety and comfort in knowing that whatever happened, we would go through it together.

The pile of desserts and side dishes was overwhelming. We had almost as much food as we did at Thanksgiving. Liam's dining room table barely had room to fit everyone around it. A tight squeeze, but no one minded.

"This was a great idea, Liam," Grant said. "Cori and I want to host as well."

Grace raised her hand. "Yes! Rotating family dinner sounds amazing. And we can always go back to the lodge if we need to."

"Well, thank you for coming," Liam said. He took my hand under the table. "And I hope I didn't screw up the lasagna too badly."

Everyone laughed.

"I'm sure it's going to be great," Kate said. Noah returned with the ice, and we began to serve.

"I'm sure it will be too," Lena called. "But if it's not, you still won't beat last Thanksgiving."

A combination of laughs and groans answered her. I got the basket of garlic bread and the side of vegetables someone had brought. Liam had the lasagna, and when we walked in, it felt like one of those holiday movies where everyone was happy and smiling.

There were no problems like cults and trials and boyfriends getting attacked and trying to find a voice that liked to disappear.

"This smells amazing, Liam," Grace said.

"Mara helped. I didn't do it alone."

I shook my head quickly. "Barely."

Lena rolled her eyes. "I don't buy that. You frosted so many cookies the other day I got ahead of schedule."

That was fun. Lena was an easy person to be around, and if what I experienced was how she treated her employees, it would be a lovely place to work.

"Did Brynn come by for an interview?"

"She did." Lena grabbed a piece of garlic bread. "She's a bit green, but very sweet. I think I'll give her a chance."

"I'm glad. Makes me feel less bad about having fewer hours," Evie said.

"Don't you dare apologize for taking care of that adorable baby."

Evie looked to the living room, where baby Avery rested in a travel crib, now asleep.

"Don't stand on ceremony," Liam said. "We never do at any other family dinner."

They didn't need to be told twice. People devoured the lasagna so quickly, we probably should have made two. The conversation flowed from one topic to the next. Plans for Emma's baby and possible names, what was happening for the ranch over the coming seasons, and some new cookie flavors Lena was thinking about.

The one thing we didn't talk about was me. Not what was happening, and not Liam and me being together. Everyone noticed, but no one said anything. Liam put his arm along the back of my chair and toyed with strands of my hair.

The tiny possessive gesture made my stomach swoop. I put my hand on his knee. Touching him in front of people was strange, but there wasn't a couple here at this table who weren't touching each other. And for the first time, no one was single. We weren't watching Jude pine after Lena or Grace battle Harlan. Everything was…perfect.

"We should go," Lucas said when we were stuffed full of both food and dessert. "We're working on it, but Avery doesn't sleep well away from home. If we don't get her back there, tonight won't be fun."

"Take care of yourselves," Daniel said. "Oh, and Mara, there was another package for you."

I went stiff.

His face was careful. "I didn't open it, but it's outside your house."

"We should go too," Jude stood and pulled Lena's chair back for her. "Besides, I'm sure Liam and Mara want some of their evening to themselves."

My cheeks turned pink, but I still smiled. Of everyone, Jude and Lena understood. She came around the table and hugged me. "You look happy."

"I am," I whispered.

"Good. I only threatened him a little the other day. You know, if you hurt my friend, I'll have Jude hurt you kind of thing."

A gasp slipped out of me. "Lena."

"What?" She laughed. "I do it for everyone. Enjoy the rest of your night."

The dishes disappeared faster than I could gather them, Noah, Grant, Kate, and Cori clearing the table and filling Liam's dishwasher. In minutes, there was nothing else for us to do.

"Thank you."

"Part of the deal." Kate winked and wrapped up what was left of her pie. "You did the cooking. Someone else does the cleaning."

Everyone leaving was more overwhelming than when they arrived. A mess of hugs and well-wishes that left me dizzy.

Liam closed the door after Grant and Cori and sighed deeply. "That went okay."

We were alone, and speaking was easier, but I was still quiet as I pressed myself into his embrace. "I think it was more than okay."

"Yeah." He tightened his hold, crushing me against him. "Thank you."

"I didn't do anything."

"Yes, you did, sweetheart."

I tucked my face into his chest, breathing him in. It amazed me how quickly his arms had become a haven. They were the only place I wanted to be.

"I know it's late, and I know you have a washing machine, but can we run to my house to grab some things?" I looked up at him and bit my lip. "Unless you don't want me to—"

Liam cut me off with a kiss, deepening it until I wasn't sure whose breath filled my lungs. The kind of kiss that led places. "If you were going to ask me if I *don't* want you to stay here, I don't want you to finish the question."

"I never want to assume."

"Assume." His voice was low. "Please assume."

So many unsaid things hung in the air between us, neither of us ready to take the leap, both of us feeling the exhilaration of walking up to the edge.

"Let's go," he said. "Quickly. Because I need to get you back here."

"Okay."

"And we can look at the package."

My stomach tumbled. There was nothing I liked about that. The last time was the veil. What would it be this time? I hoped I was overthinking and it was harmless.

But luck hadn't exactly been on my side lately.

Liam grabbed his keys, and we kept touching on the drive, despite my having to keep my seat belt on this time.

The sun was almost gone by the time we pulled up to my house. Just as Daniel said, a box sat on my front doorstep. I stared at it like it was a snake.

"I'll grab the box," he said. "You get what you need."

His words released the tension freezing my body. I got out of the truck and waited until he picked it up to unlock the door and go inside. "I can't do anything else without knowing," I said. "I wish I could."

"It's okay," Liam said. "Do you want me to open it?"

Taking a breath, I focused on the cardboard in his hands. "No, I'll do it."

Liam handed the box to me and walked with me to the couch. "I'm here with you."

I put the box on the coffee table.

No chance the contents were good. I knew they weren't. I could feel it. What I really wanted was to light a fire in the hearth and burn it without opening it. But if there was something inside that could keep Malcolm in jail? We needed to see it.

With one hand, I pried up the piece of packing tape holding the box closed. Liam's hand rested on the center of my back, a comforting presence.

At first, it didn't look like anything. Like a box of cut-up paper, scraps, and trash.

It wasn't that.

"Flowers?" I asked.

Carefully reaching inside, I lifted up a handful of destroyed flowers. Pretty blues and yellows, some shades of purple and pink. Exactly like the flowers outside my house. I moved suddenly, digging through the box in a frenzy. It held more than flowers. At the bottom was fabric. Pale and pearlescent. It, too, was shredded.

I barely had to touch it to know what it was. It was what was left of the wedding dress that had been made for me. I'd seen the designs more than I'd ever wanted to. The way it was torn looked like a wolf had run its claws through it.

Springing to my feet, I rushed outside.

"Mara," Liam called.

Spinning, I looked at my garden and the vines on my house. I knew these flowers like I knew my own body. Nothing was missing. A quick circuit of the house confirmed nothing had been touched. No one had been here cutting my flowers and dumping them into a box.

But the flowers were still the same.

Liam stood in the middle of the living room, paper in his hand. The expression on his face—

I took the paper and read the scrawled words.

You will always belong to The Family.

"Oh god," I whispered, dropping the note. "Oh *god*."

Everything came crashing down at once. They knew

where I was. For sure, they knew where I was. They knew what kinds of *flowers* I'd planted. They wanted me back.

I should have known I would never escape from him. They said those words all the time. Once you became part of The Family, you were always a member. They would take care of you. Never let you go without.

Really, they meant they owned you. You would never be able to leave. No matter how far you ran, they would drag you back, kicking and screaming. It didn't matter what you wanted. The Family came first.

"Mara." Liam's voice penetrated the fog. "Mara, sweetheart, I need you to look at me."

Look at him? Where was he? Where was I?

"You're okay. You're with me. You're in your house."

I wasn't. I was nowhere. I was where they wanted me to be. I was in the closet. Quiet. *Shhhhhh*

"Come back to me, Mara." The words were so gentle they hurt. How could I get back to him when I couldn't find him?

What was that? I smelled something. Flowers. The kind of green scent that happened when flowers were crushed. They left sticky residue on your hands and fingers.

I breathed it in, and Liam's face resolved in front of me. He was crouched in front of me, watching me carefully. I was on the floor in my house, and I didn't remember how I'd gotten there. My body felt weak—like I'd run miles without water.

The box. We'd come to get some clothes, and there was the box. "They're never going to stop," I said. "They know where I am now, and if he gets out, he wants me back. They're right, no one ever leaves. They only disappear. They're not going to stop."

Liam pulled me to him, lifting me off the floor and holding me to his chest before sitting on the couch.

"They're not going to do anything to you, Mara. Not while I'm here."

"They will," I said. "They'll send more people to attack you."

"I don't care."

I shoved my face into his shirt. "You should. I don't want them to hurt you. I don't want to go back, but if it's just me, I'm the only one who gets hurt. They can't come here. They'll hurt you. What if they hurt someone else? What if they find baby Avery or Emma? I shouldn't be here." The words spilled out of me incoherently. They weren't really words to me—just thoughts.

Dread spread across the landscape of my mind, drying up all the possibilities and paths into the future. No one ever got out. Not even Mom.

I never knew what had happened to my mother, and the deepest part of me told me I didn't want to know. Only pain lay down that path.

"Mara," Liam said, lifting me and arranging me so I straddled his lap. He took my face in his hands. "Nothing is going to happen to you or me. Understand?"

I shook my head, but he held me still.

"Yes. No one here is going to let anything happen to anyone. Our family isn't like theirs. We protect our family. We don't enslave them. Nothing is going to happen to us or Emma or baby Avery. I promise."

"You can't know that."

His face hardened. "I know we've been through everything, and we're still here. And I know we'll do everything in our power to keep each other safe. Don't get me wrong, Mara. He's trying. Malcolm saw us together, and he hates it. He's trying to scare you and scare me away. But that is *not. Going. To. Happen.*"

My vision blurred with tears, which spilled over. Liam

brushed them away with his thumbs. "I'm in this with you," he said gently. "I'm not going anywhere. He doesn't scare me."

"He scares me."

"I know. But I've got you."

I gave in to the pain and fear building in my chest and cried. I'd cried when we were in Phoenix, but it was different. Those tears had been panic and sickness—a buildup of being under Malcolm's gaze and fighting memories.

This was everything else.

This was shattering.

This was every time I'd pretended everything was fine and simply stayed quiet when I'd wanted to scream and shout. Even now, my voice wasn't fully present because they'd stolen it from me.

Liam held me and didn't flinch or back away even for a second. He held me and anchored me even though I was ruining his shirt and we'd had an incredible evening with friends.

When my breath calmed enough to hiccup and allow me a little extra air, I wrapped my arms around his neck and held him tighter. "I'm sorry."

"Why?"

"It was such a nice night."

His lips warmed my temple. "It's still a nice night."

"Even with this?"

"Even with this. Do you look back on dinner and think it was terrible now?"

I shook my head slowly.

"Dinner was amazing," he said. "And getting to be there for you—hold you—when you need me to is no hardship."

I clung to him a little harder.

"Tomorrow," he said. "We'll tell Daniel, Jude, and your lawyer about the box. Okay? They'll find what they can, and hopefully it's enough to prove he intimidated you and keep him in jail."

Gently, he pulled me in and kissed me. "Let's get what you need. I want to take you home and hold you where you can relax and sleep."

That sounded nice.

It took me a few minutes before I could make myself let him go and stand. But Liam was with me every step of the way, just like he promised he would be.

Chapter 20

Liam

I HIT the punching bag as hard as I could, letting loose every ounce of anger, frustration, and fear inside.

Mara was with Lena, and Jude was at the bakery as well. He'd seen the look on my face after we met with him and Daniel and had sent me here.

He was right.

Last night, I didn't lie. Malcolm didn't scare me, and I was fully in this with Mara. I wasn't going anywhere. But that didn't mean seeing and feeling Mara cry like the world was ending didn't piss me the fuck off.

She'd done nothing wrong, and she was paying the price over and over again.

There were no new leads as of this morning, but they were digging deeper. Trying to see if the Phoenix Police had identified any suspects in my attack. Mara's lawyer knew and was going to submit the photos we took of the box, flowers, fabric, and note to the court.

The look on Novic's face when he'd seen me…

It still unsettled me.

I only spent ten minutes in the same room, and he gave me the creeps. Madness lived in that man's eyes, plain for anyone to see.

The door opened, and Lucas walked in. I kept pounding the bag in front of me. He wasn't dressed to work out, so he was here for me. And he could talk to me. I wasn't sure I was in the mood to answer.

This dark, bleak feeling had to stay in the gym. Before I left here, I needed to be clear. Mara wasn't going to feel any of this from me. She had enough going on in her head, and I was determined not to add to it.

The whisper of fear underneath those thoughts rose, and I shoved it away. Breathed it out. Mara wasn't going to abandon me because I was scared for her. I knew it, but the terror of it had a grip on my lungs so tight I couldn't shake it.

Lucas leaned against the nearby support pole and watched as I beat the bag into submission. If the bag happened to have Malcolm's face, and the masked faces of my attackers, then so be it.

"You okay?"

I glanced at him. "Why wouldn't I be okay?"

He huffed a laugh. "First, because Jude is watching your woman so you can beat the shit out of some nonexistent enemies. Second, of all the people in the world, I understand what it's like to be in love with a woman who's being stalked."

I caught the bag and stopped it from swinging.

Stalking.

It hadn't hit me in that way before. Because Malcolm was in jail, it wasn't the same as when Evelyn's ex had stalked her. But he still knew where she was and had clearly arranged the deliveries.

They hadn't made it onto the property. We confirmed with all the cameras, including the ones I'd installed for Mara, no one had been near her house. It didn't matter, though. They still violated her peace.

"Fuck."

"Yeah, I remember that feeling."

I stripped the gloves off my hands. "I'm a soldier," I said. "I know how to attack pretty much everyone and everything. But I can't protect her from someone who essentially doesn't exist."

He chuckled. "I understand that too."

"The bastard is in jail. As far as I'm concerned, I'll do whatever I can to help him stay there. But if he can do this now, Mara is right. He's not going to stop whether he's in jail or not."

"He doesn't know where your house is," Lucas said with a shrug. "At least for now."

I looked at him and shook my head. "Whether he knows or not, it doesn't help her now. She—" I had to clear my throat. "She thinks she should give in. To protect me. And Avery and Emma. She's terrified they're going to show up and hurt someone else. Specifically, the children, like she was when they hurt her."

"That's not going to happen." His voice was low and urgent. "We have plans in place if we need them. You know that."

Every man at the ranch had an escape route planned for himself and his partner. In Lucas's and Daniel's cases, their children as well. We kept them under the radar, because an escape plan meant nothing if the entire world knew about it.

I hadn't needed one until now.

My knees shook, and I dropped into a crouch, pressing

the heels of my hands into my eyes. "I'm never going to unhear the way she cried, Lucas."

"Believe me, I get it. I still wake up thinking she's gone and I have to unearth that fucking coffin."

Evelyn's stalker of an ex-fiancé had buried her alive. We'd barely found her in time.

"Is she okay?" I asked. "Evie, after all this time?"

"She has her good days and bad days, like we all do. Is she *okay*? Yeah, I would say so. But it's not something she'll ever be able to leave behind when she sees his wounds all over her body in the mirror."

Walking over to my locker, I took out my shirt and put it back on. "I'll be honest, it's a relief to see the two of you so happy. You've both dealt with everything and come through it. That feels…very far away right now."

"It's not easy," Lucas said. "No relationship is easy. Yes, we are happy. Happier than I ever fucking thought I could be. But we have our struggles. You and Mara are going to have struggles too. All I can tell you is it is worth the work."

"You say we're going to have our struggles like—"

Lucas cut me off with a laugh. "Like you're going to be together forever? Yeah, no shit. Because I see the way you look at her. It's the way Jude looks at Lena. And Grant looks at Cori. Like I look at Evie. Every single one of us. Like they're the sun and we're the earth revolving around them. You're in love with that woman, Liam."

I blew out a breath. "I know."

He laughed. "After family dinner? Everyone knows."

"I haven't told her yet. It hasn't felt right."

"You'll know when it is. There won't be any doubt." Lucas paused and sighed. "It might feel strange, but you know everything you need to help Mara. You're not her therapist, and you shouldn't be. But you understand what it is to have trauma. Hers is just different from ours."

All of us knew. Still, the thought of Mara having to go through any of it made me want to put the gloves back on and start all over.

Taking a sip from my water bottle, I debated whether to voice the next bit. But Lucas would understand, and I needed to say it to someone.

"I'm nervous," I finally said.

"Why?"

I gestured widely to the world at large. "Because I've been here. I've seen what all of you have been through, and it's never looked like a fun place to be. And now that *I'm* here, I know it's not. All I want to do is protect Mara and love her as best as I can.

"I'm not afraid of this asshole coming after me. Or of him at all. But all I can think is, 'What if I can't protect her?'"

"God, I know that feeling." Lucas walked with me. I was done working out now. I wanted to get back to her. "When Evie first got here, I knew something was wrong, but I didn't know what. Once I knew she was in danger? I didn't want to let her out of my sight. I drove the perimeter of the ranch like a maniac, making sure we were secure, and I thought we were. If I could go back and do it again, I would make sure we had everything in place before she ever got here. The cameras, the upgraded fence, everything we didn't have.

"We had good reasons for it, but knowing what we do now? It's what I would change. You have all of it. Mara is safe on the ranch, and I got a glimpse of your security system at dinner. You've got your house on lockdown."

We all did. None of us played around with security, given the things that had happened to us before we'd ever reached Montana.

"Everyone is behind you, Liam. All you can do is take it one day at a time. And enjoy every second with her."

We'd reached my truck. "Thank you."

He put a hand on my shoulder. "Any time."

I shut the door and leaned my head back against the headrest. Everything Lucas said was true. People were behind me and would help me keep Mara safe. Help keep me safe. We weren't alone, and we could only take it one day at a time.

But most importantly, and the thing still ringing in my head, I was in love with Mara Greene.

Chapter 21

Mara

I WALKED down the street to Deja Brew from Rayne's office. Liam was meeting me there. He hadn't wanted me to walk the couple of blocks, but I had my phone, and everyone was already on alert.

Still, I made sure to pay attention to everything around me. All seemed normal in Garnet Bend. It struck me as funny how, on the surface, things could appear so normal but *feel* like you were living in an entirely different place.

I pushed open the door to Deja Brew and stopped for a second. Brynn stood behind the counter in one of the shop aprons. Her eyes lit up when she saw me. "Hi! I was hoping I would see you at some point."

"Hey." My voice came easily. It had been better the last few days. Between spending so much time with Liam and the work I was doing with Rayne, the past had a looser hold on me. Even while waiting to hear about Malcolm and his hearing.

"If I saw you again," Brynn said, "I was going to ask if we could have coffee sometime. Since I'm new and don't have a lot of friends. But I wasn't sure if asking someone you literally ran into at your therapist's office for a friendship was too weird."

I smiled and gestured around us. "Well, you don't have to ask me for coffee since we're already here."

"True."

"However," I said. "I'd like that. Talking is…hard for me. But I would like to try."

"Hey, Mara," Lena said, peeking her head out of the kitchen. "You want your usual?"

"Yes, please."

She came out and touched Brynn on the shoulder. "I'll teach you how to make it. It's something we make a lot for people."

"Awesome." Brynn looked at me. "And thanks. We'll have to figure out a time."

I nodded and retreated to the couches while Lena taught Brynn how to make the drink. Liam would be here any minute. I hoped he would be here by the time Claire called. Today, we would find out what the panel had decided about Malcolm and his parole, whether they would hear testimony again, or if he would be outright approved or denied.

"Here you go." Brynn set my drink on the table in front of me. "I hope it's all right, first time making it."

"I'm sure it's great."

The bell over the door chimed, and Liam came in, eyes locking on me. A little over an hour since he'd dropped me off at Rayne's office, and my chest still filled with happiness and relief. His gaze roved over my body like he needed to make sure I was safe and whole, even though I'd only been alone for two blocks.

Brynn looked where I was looking, and I saw her tense

up. Liam noticed her, and her reaction, and took the long way to get to me. I stood and let him pull me into his arms. "Hey," he murmured.

"Hi." I felt Brynn's eyes on us. "Um, this is Brynn."

"Hello," Liam said.

"Enjoy your drink," she said, excusing herself back to the counter.

Liam sat and pulled me down with him. "Who is that?"

"Evie and Lena were talking about her at dinner. New in town. Needed a job, so Lena's giving her a shot."

"Seems nervous."

I leaned my head on his shoulder. "New in town and alone. It sounds familiar."

"Yeah." He snaked his arm behind me and curled around my hip. "We'll keep an eye on her."

"She wants to have coffee. Be friends."

He laughed. "After one meeting? Look at you, making friends."

Leaning forward and picking up my drink, I shook my head. "No, I met her the day the veil arrived. She's one of Rayne's clients too. I was…panicking, and she ran into me outside the office."

"The day the veil was delivered?" Liam looked over our shoulders. "That's odd."

The drink she made *was* good. No difference from when Lena made it that I could tell. "Why?"

"Probably nothing," he said. "But someone you've never met before running into you on the day you get blindsided with an anonymous package from your past? It's a bit convenient."

I hadn't even thought about that. "I don't think she arrived in town the same day. It's probably a coincidence."

"Maybe."

Before I could ask him what he wanted to do, my phone rang. Claire's name was on the screen.

"Let's go outside," he said.

We stepped into the afternoon sun, and I put the call on speaker. "Claire?"

"Hey, Mara. How are you holding up?"

I looked at Liam and smiled. "I'm doing really well, thank you."

"I'm glad to hear it. Look," she sighed. "It is good news. They haven't made a decision about Malcolm's parole because they feel like the hearing was compromised. They're reconvening next week."

Hesitating, I looked at Liam, and he looked confused too. "If it's good news, why don't you sound happy?"

"The panel is offering you another chance to testify, especially in light of the second package sent to your house. But Mara, what happened last time *can't* happen again."

"It won't."

"Are you sure? Because I would rather risk a hearing without your testimony than another meltdown."

A frustrated sound leaked out of Liam, and I put my hand on his arm. I locked eyes with him. This didn't scare me right now. He was with me. My friends were with me. I could do this. "As much as I love to hear you be sympathetic about what I've gone through, Claire, I can do this. Please email me all the details and expect me there."

Silence stretched out over the line. "Shit, I'm sorry, Mara. That was really insensitive."

"Yes, it was."

"I just really want him to stay there."

I leaned into Liam. "And I'm with you. I'll see you next week."

"Okay." Her voice was a little shaky. She was still nervous. "I'll send you the details now."

"Thank you."

I'd barely ended the call before Liam's mouth was on mine. Laughter bubbled up out of me. "Lena's going to kill you if you use me to smudge the windows."

"I can take it," he whispered.

Another laugh turned into a moan when he tilted my head and kissed me deeper. I pulled back. "Liam, if you're going to kiss me like that, you can't do it in public."

He raised an eyebrow. "Oh?"

"I know I'm new to this whole sex thing, but even I know I'm not allowed to strip you down and let you have your way with me on the Main Street sidewalk."

Liam burst out laughing before hugging me so tightly my feet lifted off the ground. "I'm just so proud of you," he said. "The whole phone call. You did all the talking, you didn't hesitate, and you stood up for yourself. It was incredible, sweetheart."

"I did do that, didn't I?" Closing my eyes, I enjoyed the combined warmth of both him and the late-summer sun. "I guess it helps when I'm spending all my time with someone who makes talking easy."

We went back inside, Liam tugging me down beside him. "I'm glad you can talk with me. And I'm glad you feel it's easier. But it makes me a little sad too."

"Why?"

He brushed a piece of hair behind my ear. "Because if I hadn't waited so long, maybe it could have been easier sooner."

I let the words sink through me as I took another sip of my coffee. "I don't know. Maybe it would have, and maybe it wouldn't have. Today is a good day. But it's still not easy."

"I know."

"You and I," I said and gestured between us, "we already

have too many things in our past to worry about with adding another one."

"Hey, Liam!" Lena called. "You want coffee?"

"No thanks," he called back. Then lower, he added, "There's something else I want so much more than coffee."

I blushed and looked away. It was a whole new world with him like this. Who knew if I would ever get used to comments like that one, or if my body would stop reacting by turning my whole face and chest bright red. But as I told him, we already had too many things to worry about. The amazing thing happening between us? No reason to add anything to it.

"Take me home?" I asked.

"Absolutely."

I waved to Brynn, and she smiled, though she still looked at Liam with wariness.

His truck was parked a little down the street. "I'm sorry we have to go again," I said. "To Phoenix. If you're coming with me."

"Sweetheart, there's no way I'm staying here for that. I want to see you kick some ass."

"I don't know about that. I'm still nervous, despite what I said to Claire. It feels good, though, too, and I think I can do it."

"You can." He boosted me up into the truck and made his way to the other side. "I know you can."

One breath in and one breath out. I was glad I would have a second chance. Malcolm was the last person I wanted to face again, but he needed to be in jail, and I was grateful I had another opportunity to keep him there.

Chapter 22

Liam

"HOW WAS THAT?" Mara asked.

"I think it was perfect."

We sat in my living room, practicing Mara's statement for the hearing. Listening to what she'd gone through—the beatings and fear—and what she'd narrowly escaped, never ceased to make my hands clench into fists. But we got to the point where her voice didn't waver. She could go through the details and not break.

It would be different with Malcolm there, but I knew she could do it. I would be there too. This time, I wouldn't let her be afraid. She would keep her eyes on me and ignore everyone else.

"Really?"

"Yes. Absolutely."

Mara's eyes shone, and she came over to me and climbed on top of me on the couch. The last few days, we'd had nothing to do but spend time with each other, and more than ever, I knew I was head over heels in love with this woman.

I loved everything about her, including who she was when I met her. I loved her silent, and I loved her loud. But watching her bloom and gain confidence, watching her *speak*, was one of the most beautiful things I'd ever seen.

She kissed me, and our mouths kept slipping apart because I couldn't stop smiling.

"I can't kiss you when you're laughing."

"I'm not laughing. I'm smiling."

It was her turn to laugh. "Well, stop that."

"Yes, ma'am."

I slid my hands up the sides of her hips and under her shirt, savoring the feeling of her skin. I would never get enough. "We should do this instead of packing."

She groaned. "Don't remind me."

"I need to remind you," I said. "Or rather, I need to remind both of us."

Our flight to Phoenix left in the early afternoon. Whether we wanted to pack or not, both of us would rather have a stress-free day than leave it to the last minute.

"Can we do both?" Mara asked.

The way she looked up at me and bit her lip, *fuck*. I was already holding myself back from laying her out on the couch and devouring her. "We can absolutely do both." My voice rasped like I'd been yelling. "The question is, before or after?"

Mara's eyes sparkled with mischief. "We can do both of that, too."

I moaned into her neck. "You're going to kill me, you know that?"

"You can't die. If you die, then we can't do *both*."

Gripping her thighs, I stood and carried her up the stairs.

We weren't waiting anymore, and for what I had planned, I wanted the bed and not the couch.

She tasted like the fruit in the summertime, light and sweet and delicious. I kicked the bedroom door open, and we tumbled onto the bed together. We weren't even going to make it to taking all our clothes off.

"I want to try something," she whispered.

"Anything."

Mara turned over, pressing her back into my chest. Until now, we'd done nothing but the basics, and I didn't care because it was *incredible*. "Like this. Is that okay?"

"Mara, I can't think of anything you'd want to try that I wouldn't be okay with. No matter what, I'm going to make you see stars."

Her whimper nearly made me go blind. "Yes, please."

"Hold on, sweetheart."

———

I BRUSHED Mara's hair off her neck, letting the strands fall through my fingers. Our breath was coming back to us, but I didn't want to move yet.

"Was it worth trying?"

Mara arched her back, pushing her body into mine, and I had my answer. "Yes. Yes, it was."

She turned over and snuggled closer. "I want to try everything with you."

"We can do that." I sank the same hand into her hair and gently pulled her head back so I could kiss her neck. "We'll have to spend a lot more time in bed, though."

"You say that like it's a problem."

"Definitely not," I murmured the words into her skin. "Just making sure you know, so when I lock you in here with me, I can say I warned you."

She laughed, breathless. "As long as we hydrate."

God, I loved this woman.

Mara sighed and stretched. "I don't want to move."

"Then don't."

"I have to. I need to pack. Or repack." Her suitcase still sat at the end of my bed, filled with clothes.

I pulled her in, heart pounding. This was a risk, and I still wanted it. "When we get back from Phoenix," I whispered. "Will you come back here?"

"Yes." She took a breath. "If that's okay. We still don't know who sent me the boxes, and…I like being here with you."

"I was going to ask when you came back here, if you'd just like to unpack."

Her little gasp terrified me as much as it gave me hope.

"Your cabin is beautiful," I said. "And I understand if you don't want to leave it. But I can see you here. I can see your flowers outside and your ivy climbing up the side of the house. I can see your clothes in the closet, and your toothbrush already lives next to mine.

"Most of all, I can see going to sleep with you every night and waking up with you every morning."

I pulled her back so I could see all of her face, and her eyes were wide and glassy with tears. Lucas said it would feel right, and it did. Now was the time. "I'm falling in love with you, Mara Greene. I know it's a big thing to say, and I don't expect you to say it back. But I need to tell you. I don't even think I'm falling anymore. I am *in* love with you. I want a future with you. I want to make a home with you, and no matter what happens, I want you with me."

Her mouth opened, and no sound came out. I grinned and kissed her. For once, I was glad she was speechless. It was a good sign.

Mara reached out. She moved her hands and arms and

legs to wrap around me entirely and buried her face in my neck. I'd never felt more at peace than in this moment with her. The fear of failure was still there, but as long as I was holding Mara, nothing else mattered.

"Is that a yes?" I asked softly.

She nodded and tapped her fingers on my back. Two taps. Two taps. Two taps.

Packing could wait. I rolled Mara beneath me and kissed her. We needed each other far more than we needed clothes. Or to pack. We needed this more than we needed *breath*.

"Liam," she whispered and shook her head. "My voice."

"I know." It would still disappear, especially when she was overwhelmed. "You're still speaking to me, sweetheart. I hear you."

Two taps.

We didn't need any more words for me to show her how in love with her I was.

Mara

I WAS A PENDULUM. The entire day, I swung back and forth between confidence and nerves. When we stopped by Deja Brew for coffee, I felt great, and both Brynn and Lena wished me luck.

To test Liam's suspicions, I mentioned where we were going, but she didn't react in any particular way.

By the time we got to the airport, I was questioning everything again. Now we were in Phoenix and my stomach was settled, but it could turn back any second. Liam was the one keeping the real nerves at bay.

I'm falling in love with you, Mara Greene.
I don't even think I'm falling anymore. I am in *love with you.*

His words echoed on repeat through my head all day. A nice, beautiful thing to hear when I was worried about the testimony in the morning, and I didn't have to speak for Liam to understand. He knew me now, and I knew him.

We stayed in the same hotel, but this time, there was only one room and one bed for us to share. Anything else was unacceptable. The two of us were a unit. For the first time, I believed it wasn't going to change.

I am in love with you.

Was I in love with Liam?

My gut said yes, but how did I know? Being in love wasn't something I planned for or imagined. I trusted Liam. I felt safe with him. He would never hurt me intentionally. But love?

My chest warmed with the word. Love might be the big, intangible thing that pulled me toward him like a magnet. The way my stomach tumbled when he looked at me or when he placed his hand on the small of my back. When he pulled me close in places like the airport simply to make sure I wasn't brushing up against strangers in a crowd.

Maybe love was looking at him across this hotel room and feeling all the attraction in the world and wanting so much more than his body. I wanted his mind and his heart. I wanted all of him.

"How about room service tonight?" he asked.

It was a sweet gesture, and we both knew the truth of it. Room service meant neither of us had to leave the hotel, and it also meant not letting anyone outside of the hotel know where we were staying.

Even if they met us in the lobby, it was still a risk we didn't want to take after last time.

Liam came to me, and I tapped him twice on the shoulder. Room service was good. "Let's look at the menu," he said, leaving me only long enough to get the menu from the desk.

He ordered a burger, and I had some pasta while we watched a silly sitcom on TV. I rarely watched TV at home. I didn't have one. I could watch on my laptop, but I never felt like it was needed. But the antics of the characters were distracting in the perfect way.

I could do this, and I knew it. But seeing Malcolm again, and the emotional memory of falling apart, had me on edge.

The show ended, and Liam turned off the TV, taking our dishes and setting them outside in the hallway on the tray before coming back to me.

"Do you have your voice right now?" He sat down next to me again.

"A little."

He smiled. "Can you talk to me?"

"I'm nervous to see him again."

"You're not going to look at him," Liam said gently. "You're only going to look at me."

"I know." I could only manage a whisper. "But I'm still going to feel him looking at me. I'm still going to remember everything he did and wanted to do."

Liam reached out and tucked a strand of hair behind my ear. "What can I do to make it better?"

I scooted toward him on the bed. "I don't want to think about it," I said, leaning my forehead on his shoulder. "I know I should probably run through things again, but more than anything, I just want to pretend like it's not happening. Like we're at home and going to bed."

He grinned. "I like it when you say *at home*."

My whole face flushed. I couldn't believe I was going to move in with him. It felt so right, and I didn't want anything else. Ever.

Oh my god, I *was* in love with him. There wasn't any

other explanation. Butterflies rioted in my stomach. I leaned forward and kissed him, driven by both my realization and the need not to think about anything but this moment.

"That kind of going to bed?" he teased.

"Yes."

One hand slipped behind my neck to pull me closer and deepen our kiss. I'd learned with him. I knew the kind of roller coaster kissing could take you on, especially with tongues involved.

And every time, we got better.

We sank down onto the bed together. "I want to try something," I said against his lips.

"Hmm?" Liam moved to kiss my neck. "Something new already? You're going wild."

"Maybe I've always been wild and didn't know."

"Sweetheart, you can be wild all you want. You already drive me wild."

I laughed, but it turned into a breathless moan under lips and hands. "That was cheesy."

"And you loved every second."

Our clothes came off piece by piece. I never got tired of seeing Liam revealed. What felt like miles of perfect skin and muscles that flexed and contracted under my touch. I could trace them, following the lines.

"What did you want to try?"

Instead of telling him, I showed him. I rolled, so I straddled his hips on the bed and smiled down at him. His eyes were full of both lust and amusement. "I see. There are definite advantages to this."

Before I could ask him what, he lifted me. His strength never failed to make my jaw drop. Lifted me up and up before lowering me…directly over his face.

"Liam?"

His chuckle vibrated against me, and I gasped. "Brace

yourself." I didn't need to ask what for. His mouth and tongue were on me in that way he had that made me see stars. But like this? Why did it feel so different?

I braced my hands on the headboard, sinking into the pleasure he offered and savoring every second.

Liam held me against his mouth, as relentless as he was gentle. An impossible contradiction driving me higher. He knew *exactly* what my body responded to now and never hesitated to use it for my benefit. The way his tongue curled and the subtle, pulsing rhythm drawing me closer to that bright peak of pleasure.

I dove off the edge and straight into it, shuddering and gasping. My voice didn't make itself known like this, but Liam never minded. He claimed my entire body spoke to him.

Lifting me again, he dragged me back down, and we came together with a groan. His mouth shone in the hotel light with everything he'd just tasted of me. And now, on top of him, I could barely breathe.

How the smallest changes in position could make things feel new and better and brighter, I wasn't sure. But I liked the way this felt. I liked how deep he was. I loved being able to see the look on his face. I loved how powerful I felt as I rocked into him and he thrust back.

We'd connected before this hotel, but it was here when he'd first held me through the night. In a way, it felt like this place was the true start of our journey.

Liam dug his fingers into my hips, guiding me, helping me, bringing me down onto him over and over again until I was on the edge, ready to give in and break. He played my body like the finest instrument, and I never wanted anybody else to try.

A few flicks of his fingers, and I collapsed onto his chest in pleasure. Our mouths met, hungry and wanton, the shining aftermath inside me drawn out by him seeking his own climax.

I loved this part. The desperate moments after he drove me to pleasure and before he found his own. Everything was glossy and shining, the orgasm still flickering through my body like a thousand fireworks.

Liam held me close, finishing with my name on his lips before we both caught our breath, sharing each other's air with soft kisses.

He rolled us to the side and froze. "We went so fast, I forgot the condom."

Part of me expected to feel terror or regret, but…I didn't. It felt right. There was nothing between us now, and I liked it that way. We hadn't talked about it yet, our future, but I saw it.

I wanted kids. A baby who was half Liam and half me? I nearly teared up at the thought. My soul desired the vision so fiercely, it stole my breath.

"It's okay," I whispered.

He settled his hand around my hip. "I haven't been with anyone else in years."

I smirked and kissed him. "I think I have you beat."

Liam chuckled and pulled me closer. This was exactly where I wanted to be.

Before I fell asleep, I tapped Liam's skin three times. He tapped back the same pattern—the meaning clear to both of us. Words weren't necessary.

Chapter 23

Mara

MALCOLM STARED at me from across the room. I felt it where I sat next to Liam. But as we planned, I didn't look at or acknowledge him at all. He didn't deserve my time or attention. The only reason I was here was because of things he'd done.

He didn't hold power over me anymore.

"Miss Greene," one of the panel members said. "Are you prepared to speak?"

My stomach swam with sickness and nerves, but I nodded. Liam leaned over and kissed my cheek. "You have this," he said softly. "If you need me, I'm right here."

I squeezed his hand twice.

Claire smiled tightly as I made my way to the front of the courtroom where I'd been last time. She was nervous and had a right to be. But despite the nausea in my gut, I was calm.

"Miss Greene, it's nice to see you again," a man on the

panel said. "If you would, please tell us your experience with Mr. Novic in your own words."

Here we go. I took a breath and looked at Liam. Malcolm was there, but only in the background. He didn't exist. He was nothing.

"I don't remember joining The Family," I said. "I was six. My earliest memories are of the compound. In general, we lived a simple life. I was with the children and my mother. Sometimes, I saw my brother. But he left the compound when I was ten, and I never saw him again."

Claire stood, looking relieved. "Do you know what happened to your brother?"

I shook my head. "No."

She gestured. "Please, continue."

Slowly, I did, outlining the things she'd asked me about the daily life of The Family as I grew older. The chores, the beatings, the forced silence.

Liam nodded in encouragement. "My mother was paired off with a man—I don't remember his name, but she was planning to leave. She told me once, very quietly, and made me promise not to tell anyone. We were going to leave together and have a better life. Three days later, she disappeared. No one even acted like she was gone. She simply…evaporated."

"And you never saw her again?" Claire asked.

"No."

"And how do you know your mother didn't run away and simply leave you behind?" she asked.

I blinked. It wasn't a question I'd prepared for. "I don't," I said honestly. "But she wasn't the only woman to disappear."

"But you have no proof she didn't run?"

My voice shook. "No. However, given what I know of Mr. Novic and what he planned for me, I have no doubt he and the other men in The Family are responsible for her disappearance."

I kept going. "Two years after my mother disappeared, Malcolm called me into his office and informed me I had been chosen as a bride of honor. There were others. Girls my age who married Malcolm, but not only him. Brides of honor were married to The Family itself. So, every man was her husband and had husband's rights. The other girls who tried to fight came back with bruises and broken bones.

"After that, no one fought."

Claire stood once again. "But you weren't forced to become one?"

"No," I said. "The process involved the women and girls of The Family embroidering a dress and veil. It took a long time. Luckily for me, the compound was raided before mine were complete. But it's the same veil that arrived at my home."

"And what would have happened if you hadn't been rescued?"

I looked at Liam and noted the pride in his eyes. "I have no doubt if the compound hadn't been raided, Malcolm would have forced me to marry him and allowed the men of The Family to rape me at will."

The already quiet courtroom went dead silent.

"You said you received another package?"

"Yes." My hands were shaking with adrenaline now. "What remained of the wedding dress, torn to pieces, along with many cut-up flowers that match the ones planted outside my home. There was also a note which read, 'You will always belong to The Family.' So, I have no doubt, if released, Malcolm Novic would attempt to reinstate The Family, along with all its practices."

"Thank you very much for your testimony, Miss Greene," Claire said. "It has been very insightful."

"Yes," the same panel member who welcomed me agreed. "It has. You may step down, Miss Greene."

It was over, and I took the risk. I looked at Malcolm. Rage contorted his features. He didn't even try to hide it. It was easier to walk past him again and back to Liam, who tucked me into his side and leaned his head against mine. "You were amazing."

"Thank you."

Even with my newfound love of words, it was still a lot to speak so much in front of this many people. I leaned against him, exhausted.

I couldn't even listen to the panel while they asked for more testimony and found there wasn't any. Malcolm would speak to the panel himself, but I wasn't going to stay and listen to that.

"We'll reconvene in ten minutes."

Claire followed us out the doors. "You were incredible, Mara. Thank you. I don't think there's anything he can say to save himself now. I'll stay and listen, but they'll make their decision and announce tomorrow. I'll text you the rest of the details when we're finished."

"Thank you," I said.

"No. Seriously, thank *you*." She was smiling. "Because of you, he's never going to get out. And that's incredible. You did a good thing, Mara."

She waved and spun back into the courtroom like the whirlwind she was. I still felt like I was standing motionless in the middle of a chaotic storm.

"She's right," Liam said. "But I don't know if you want to keep hearing it."

"Not right now," I admitted.

He chuckled and kissed my temple. "Let's get the hell out of here. I think you've more than earned some ice cream, don't you?"

"Oh my god, yes."

Liam took my hand, and we went in search of Phoenix's best ice cream, and I felt a thousand pounds lighter.

———

"WELL, THAT'S NOT GOOD."

The engine in our rental car made a noise I knew no engine should make. You didn't have to be a mechanic to know that. The court session for the announcement started in fifteen minutes. While the building was close, it wasn't *that* close. Even calling a cab would make us late.

"It's okay," I said. "I don't need to see it."

"Yes, you do," Liam said. "You need to be able to look that fucker in the eye when they tell him he's going back to jail. I want that for you."

I wanted it to, but we couldn't have everything.

"Call Claire," Liam said. "Maybe she can come over and pick you up."

"Me?" I said, heart picking up. "Just me?"

He looked torn. "I need to figure out what's wrong with the car in order to get it back to the airport. Either getting under the hood myself, or calling the rental company and having them send a replacement. It will take time."

I heard what he wasn't saying. Our flights were the last ones that could get us to Missoula today, so unless we wanted to spend another night, this needed to be fixed. If there was one thing I knew, it was that both of us desperately wanted to be home. Arizona may have been my home for a long time, but it wasn't anymore. Montana was my home.

Liam was my home.

"Is it safe?" I asked.

His lips tightened into a line. "With Claire? Yes. Once you're in the courthouse, they won't touch you. No one will risk adding to Malcolm's sentence or catching one of their own."

And notably, none of the angry men who'd been with Malcolm last time were in the courtroom yesterday. I pulled out my phone and called Claire.

"Hello? Mara? Where are you?"

"Our car died at the hotel. Can you come get me?"

She didn't even question it. "I'll be right there."

The line went dead.

"Okay. She's coming."

Liam still looked torn. "I should come with you. We can stay another night."

"I want to go home," I told him. "This is easy. It's just listening to people talk. And you're right, inside the courthouse, everything is fine. Malcolm can only do so much while he's in handcuffs in a courthouse."

One more long breath, and he nodded. "Don't leave the courthouse without calling me," he said. "I'm going to take care of this as quickly as possible."

"Maybe we'll be done before you are," I said, leaning across the seat to kiss him. "I feel good. I promise."

He caught me and kissed me hard, a wordless reminder of everything between us.

"There she is," he said.

I looked over my shoulder. Claire had pulled up next to us. Reaching out, I tapped his hand three times. "See you soon."

"I love you," he told me.

My gut fluttered, and I was grinning like a fool as I slid into Claire's car. "Sorry about this."

"Hell of a way to start the day," she smiled. "But things happen. Let's just get there. I can't wait to watch him go down."

I couldn't agree more.

Chapter 24

Liam

NOTHING I SAW under the hood made sense. It seemed like the car should be working, but it *very* distinctly wasn't.

Finally, I called the rental place. As much as the puzzle lover in me wanted to figure out what was wrong, I wanted to get this over with more. So Mara and I could go home and leave all of this behind. She would still struggle, and so would I, but we would have each other, and that was everything.

A car pulled up next to the rental, and the guy waved before he got out. "Hey. I'm Dave. Sorry about this."

"Thank you for coming so quickly."

He laughed. "Believe me, if there's a problem with the car, they want it fixed fast. Turn her over for me?"

I slid back into the driver's seat and turned the key in the ignition. It sputtered like it was *trying* to start, but there was no life in it. If anything, it sounded like it was on its last legs.

"I took a look," I said. "I do some tune-up work on trucks, and nothing stood out to me. I'm stumped."

"Yeah. Wow. Can't say I've heard a car make that noise. Like…ever. Okay."

He poked his head under the hood and did exactly what I'd done. It didn't look like he had more of an idea than I did, which fed my primal male satisfaction in a way I would never admit to anyone.

Dave suddenly went rigid with shock before looking at something closer. "What the hell?"

"You found something?"

"I don't know. Hold on." He ducked down and looked underneath the car. "Shit." He reappeared and came around the car, flipping open the gas cap. I watched as he ran his fingers around the inside and smelled them. "Yeah, it's not something wrong with the engine. Or, I guess it is, but it's not *because* of the engine."

I shook my head. "What do you mean?"

"I mean, you've got water in your gas tank. Like a whole shit-ton of water in there. It's leaking out below. No wonder the car won't start. There's barely any gas in there at all, and the engine is probably fried since you've been trying to start it for a bit."

Staring at him, I tried to put the pieces together. "Water in the gas tank?"

He laughed and clapped me on the shoulder. "You must have someone who really hates you in order to do that. And at the same time, you're lucky it's a rental."

Every instinct I had screamed at me. Someone had done this. Last night, after we'd returned to the hotel, someone had siphoned the gas out of the tank and replaced it with water. If Mara weren't with Claire right now, I would be losing my shit.

Why would they do this? What purpose would it serve?

Just to stall us? Fuck with us? I didn't know, and I didn't want to find out.

"What do I need to do for the car?" I asked, my mind barely present in the interaction.

Dave held out a different set of keys. "I'll take care of it. You take the one I came in, and I hope you have a good rest of the day."

"That's it?"

"That's it."

I swallowed, resisting the urge to drive to the courthouse at sixty miles an hour. "I'm sorry about this. I don't know how it happened."

He waved a hand and pulled out his phone, holding it up to his ear. "They'll be pissed, but that's what insurance is for. I'm sure they'll call you later. Yeah," he answered whoever was on the other line. "We're going to need to tow this one back."

Going to the other car, I unlocked it. An easy fix, but I still didn't know why. I needed to get the hell out of here, get Mara, and call Daniel.

But first, I wanted to be able to get the hell out of town immediately. I went into the hotel and grabbed our bags, getting them into the new rental before checking out of the hotel. Mara was right. We could stay here another night, but I wanted us to be home. In *our* house. In *our* bed. Finally starting a life together.

My heart sang, and my chest vibrated with it. I'd never imagined it would happen this quickly, but when it was right, you knew. Even before, with Jenny, it hadn't felt like this. Back then, it had been new love. Good and sweet, two people who didn't understand life, wrapped up in each other and too optimistic about the reality of the world.

It wasn't like that between Mara and me. We both had suffered. We both had survived. We both understood the darkness that lurked beneath the surface. You had to choose to keep going. Choose not to let the darkness consume you. And choose the people you wanted with you on your journey through it.

Mara and I chose each other.

As far as I was concerned, she was it for me. I didn't care if she never wanted to get married because of what Malcolm had done. All I ever wanted was her. A life and a family and everything that came with it.

My only question now was how long I had to wait before I could tell her exactly that. She knew I loved her, and though she hadn't said the words out loud, she loved me. I didn't want to pressure her, and yet I wanted to get down on my knees and declare myself hers forever.

I couldn't wipe the grin off my face. We had to get home first. Rest, recover, and take a breath. Then I would plan something for the two of us. Another date. Maybe I would take her to the lake in the mountains for a long weekend. Make love to her under the stars before I asked her if she'd be my forever.

One last mental check to make sure I had everything, and I was out the door. It had been long enough, the hearing might be over by now. I paused before I got in the car, pulling out my phone, about to call Mara and check.

"Liam?" a soft, female voice said.

I startled, turning around. The woman who stood behind me was wrecked. Battered all to hell, with a black eye and a bloody lip. She held her ribs like she'd been kicked, and she was limping. But more than that, she was familiar. I'd seen her the day before yesterday. "Brynn?"

She nodded.

"What the hell are you doing here?"

Whatever it was, it wasn't good. She clearly needed a

hospital, besides the fact that she was *here* and not in Garnet Bend.

"I'm here with Neil."

My body shook, barely able to focus on her when my instincts were screaming so loudly I could hear them. "I don't know who that is."

Brynn winced. "He's the leader of The Family."

Pure, icy dread poured down my spine. "What did you just say?"

"It never stopped," she said. "Not for one second. It only ever went underground. For years. They were banking on Malcolm getting out and killing him so the ties would finally be broken and no one would know. But that changed when they realized Mara would speak up at the hearing. And even after the first session, they knew it would be enough to keep him in there. Exactly what they're announcing right now. But he won't survive the night in prison."

"How the fuck do you know that? *Why are you here?*" My voice thundered across the parking lot, drawing looks from everyone, including Dave. To her credit, Brynn didn't flinch.

"Neil took power, and he wants Mara. He was a little older than her when The Family was raided, and he wants to continue The Family's work with her. I'm here because he promised me—" Her voice broke. "He promised me I'd be with him too. Totally equal status with her. And I believed him. He was so perfect. You don't understand, he was the perfect man. And it was a lie. Once he had Mara, he was always going to kill me." She sobbed. "And now that he has her, he tried. I just managed to get away and come here. I needed to warn you. Last night, I was here when they sabotaged the car. They hoped it would work this way."

But my brain was no longer working. "What do you mean?"

"He tried to kill me. I—"

I stepped into her space. "What do you mean, now that he *has Mara*?"

She went pale. "He has her. By now, he does. Otherwise, he wouldn't have touched me. He needed me to watch her. I can't believe I was so stupid."

"Brynn." I needed her to focus. "Mara is at the courthouse right now. With her lawyer. You're telling me the man abducted her from the courthouse?"

"No," she whispered. "I'm saying she never made it to the courthouse."

Chapter 25

Mara

I DIDN'T LIKE DRIVING AWAY from Liam. We hadn't been apart for so long now, it felt unnatural. The only times we'd been separated from each other were when I stayed with Lena at Deja Brew. I'd become accustomed to him being the warm presence at my side.

But I would be okay. I knew I would. After yesterday, my confidence was higher than my nerves, but just barely. Still, I could do it. It was only listening to people, no words needed. All by itself, it was better.

Besides, maybe it was good I did this by myself. Then I knew I *could* do it by myself. I would be able to look back and say I stood on my own two feet, in the same room as Malcolm, and came out on the other side. Alive, healthy, and happy.

Claire was speaking, but I hadn't been listening, thinking about Liam. It was better he'd stayed behind so we could go home. I smiled to myself. This was what being in love was. We'd only been apart a few minutes, and I missed him.

On the way home, I wanted to plan moving my things to his house. Would Daniel be okay with it? I didn't pay rent for the cabin, as it was a perk of the job, but I hoped he wouldn't be offended I was leaving. I was still going to work at the ranch. It was my home, and that wasn't changing.

We whizzed past a stoplight I vaguely recognized. The courthouse was on our left, and we were driving right past it. The parking lot for it was around the corner, but we passed the entrance for it too.

I cleared my throat. "Sorry, Claire, I wasn't paying attention. Is everything okay?"

She glanced over at me from the driver's seat. "Of course. Why wouldn't it be?"

"The courthouse?" I asked. "You drove past it."

Laughing, she smiled. "You weren't paying attention. I said it was a good thing you called me, because I was about to call you and tell you the hearing had been moved to a different building. So it all worked out in the end."

"Oh." I blew out a breath. "Right. Why did they move it?"

"Full docket. Since this is just a notification of their decision, we got bumped for a case that needed the courtroom space more than we did. Nothing to worry about."

I wasn't worried exactly, but the unknown did make me nervous. Especially when it came to Malcolm Novic. "Do we know how big the room is going to be? I just want to be prepared in case it's small and I have to be near him."

"I don't, sorry."

"It's okay."

She sighed. "This whole thing has been ludicrous and confusing, and I will be so glad to leave it all behind."

Something we both could agree on. "I admit I'm a little

nervous. We still don't know who sent the veil and note since he had to have someone do it."

"He won't be able to send you anything else," Claire said. "Trust me."

I looked over at her. "How do you know that?"

She shrugged. "I just do." Then she shook her head like she was clearing it. "I'm sure the panel will take the packages into consideration when sending him back. They'll likely limit his access to things like communication. So he won't be able to send you anything else."

"That's…good."

Claire looked strange, and she was acting even stranger. Looking in the rearview mirror, as if she expected someone to be following us.

"But truly, it's been incredibly hard, this whole thing. Having to watch Malcolm sit there like he still has any power at all. Like he didn't throw it all away when he wasn't fucking careful enough not to get caught."

"What?"

"Back when the compound was still here in Arizona, everything could have been avoided. I've seen everything, Mara. He could have misdirected the FBI away from raiding the place. When they came, he could have had a plan in place and made everything look normal. Instead, he got cocky and fucked with *everything*."

My breath went shallow.

When the compound was still here in Arizona.

Did that mean what I thought it meant? It still existed somewhere? Daniel and Jude hadn't found anything. There wasn't any evidence, and they said the old property was mostly abandoned.

"Claire, it's a good thing it happened. You helped send him to jail the first time. You're putting him back in jail and keeping him there. This doesn't make any sense."

"I'm trying to tell you how hard it was, watching it," she said. "Watching him have to stay quiet and hidden while everyone else fawned over someone who's essentially dead. Having to stay in the shadows?" She huffed out a breath. "He deserved better. *Deserves* better. Finally, he's going to get it. It's been far too long."

"Who deserves better?" I asked quietly.

"Neil." She looked at me, eyes wild, and I barely recognized her. Claire looked like she was full of restless energy, bouncing in the seat a little and tapping her fingers on the steering wheel. "Neil deserves fucking *everything* for what Malcolm's done. When one father passes, another takes his place. What does it matter if the previous one hasn't fully passed? He's never getting out of prison. We made sure of that."

Her smile now was maniacal. I couldn't move or breathe. Every muscle was tense. I didn't even want to reach for my phone in case she saw, because she was driving, and I didn't know what she might do.

Panic began to claw at the inside of my stomach, but there was nothing I could do. Not until I could reach my phone and call Liam. Breathe in, breathe out.

I felt my voice slipping away, but I needed to hold on to it. The urge to curl in on myself and hide rose, and I fought it back. Whatever happened now, I needed to be awake, alert, and ready. Because like hell was I just *letting* this happen. I had things to live for and a man I loved waiting for me.

God, did Liam know? He hadn't called me. Please, Liam, figure it out. I was going to do everything I could to get out, but I also knew Liam would move heaven and earth to find me if he knew something was wrong.

The car sped up, and I looked outside to see us merging

onto the highway. I felt one last spark of hope. "Claire, where is the other building?"

"Just a little farther. A few exits."

Yeah, that was a lie.

Making sure I barely moved, I slid my hand down into the pocket of my jeans. Thank god my phone was on the side of the car next to the door.

"Who's Neil?" I asked, keeping my voice light and conversational.

"You don't remember him?"

I cleared my throat. "No. Should I?"

"He's a member of The Family, just like you. A few years older than you, but not by much. I would think you would know the name."

Keeping my mouth shut, I tapped the screen of my phone to wake it up. The Family kept everyone separated by sex. She knew it. It was one of the major points of The Family. But I also knew she wasn't in her right mind right now.

Sickness spun inside me. How had this happened? How had they gotten to her? After all this time? I wanted to scream, but I didn't have space for it. Instead of my voice being silent, I let the silence creep through my mind. No room for anything but thoughts to help myself get out of this.

We sped south down the highway. I didn't mention how many exits we'd passed or ask where the court building was. We both knew we weren't going there.

Down by my leg, I navigated to Liam's text message. *HELP.*

I sent it, glancing over at Claire. She didn't notice what I'd done, thankfully.

"Claire," I said quietly.

"Yes?"

"What happened?" I asked.

She drummed her hands on the wheel. "What do you mean?"

"When did you…" I swallowed down bile. "When did you become a member of The Family?"

"Years ago now. During the appeals process for Malcolm. I interviewed some older members of The Family, and everything they said…" She *glared* at me. "It was nothing like what you made it out to be. *Nothing* like what you said yesterday. How you could even think those things—"

I held my breath and looked down at my phone. No response.

"Being with The Family is a gift. Where you're treasured. Neil loves me, and I already know he loves you. We're going to be happy, Mara. I know you've struggled a lot since you were taken from us, but you're finally coming home. This is a good thing. And you'll still be a bride of honor. Neil is willing to forgive you for everything."

My knuckles were white from how hard I gripped my phone and the edge of my seat. How could she ask me things like she had in the courtroom yesterday and still be this far gone? How could I have had no idea after all this time?

What she'd said about my mother and there being no proof…

"Do you know what happened to my mother?"

"You know as well as I do once you're a part of The Family, you *always* are. Which is why you should be thankful for Neil forgiving you. He could have chosen to bury you next to her, and it would be more than you deserve."

I closed my eyes. Of course. Deep inside, I'd always known they killed her, but confirmation was different from the intangible possibility she could have gotten out and lived a normal life. I wouldn't have blamed her for leaving me if she had the chance.

Still no answer from Liam.

Please, I begged the universe. God. Whoever might be listening. *Please let him see.*

I typed out one more desperate plea.

Liam. I love you.

He knew, but if I didn't get to say the words aloud, he would have these from me.

The car slowed, pulling off an exit. This was good. If we went slowly enough, I could get out and run. All I needed was one moment and distance. I could do this. I could survive.

Claire pulled into a gas station, and relief washed over me in a cool wave. As soon as she stopped, I was gone.

She pulled up beside the pump, and I *moved*. Ripping off my seat belt, I lunged for the door and pushed it open, my momentum crumbling as I ran directly into a person. A man. Leering at me in a way that was far too familiar.

A second later, I saw the gun he held low by his waist. Pointed straight at me.

Claire ran around the car and plastered herself against him, kissing him like we weren't in public in the middle of the day. They were blocking my way out, and the gun prodded into my ribs.

"Go drive, baby," he said, and Claire smiled, her eyes glazed with adoration. His eyes once again fixed on me. He tilted his head to the side. "Nice try, but I made myself clear. You belong to us."

I needed to tell him I didn't. I would never belong *to* anyone ever again. Only *with* someone, and I'd already chosen.

My voice was gone when I needed it most.

Neil smiled. "Get in the fucking car, Mara."

Chapter 26

Liam

"PLEASE, YOU HAVE TO FIND HER," Brynn said, eyes full of tears as her hands were cuffed behind her back. The police at the courthouse took her into custody as an accessory. Because she was right.

Claire and Mara had never shown up at the announcement. Malcolm was already on his way back to prison to complete his sentence without parole, and it didn't fucking matter, because Mara *wasn't here*.

Everyone at the ranch knew, because I'd called them, nearly screaming. Now my mind was a deadly silent place. Malcolm was irrelevant. He was in custody. Brynn didn't know where Neil was, only that Claire was delivering Mara to him, and they were going to The Family's compound.

Out of the country.

Terror gripped my entire body.

If they got her across the border, she was gone. Everything changed once you left the US. Anything could happen, and you couldn't rely on government support or swiftness. And if they were smart, they'd set up camp in a country without extradition.

"Liam, you need to help her," Brynn called. They pulled her away, and I watched her leave, frozen to the spot. I was going to help Mara, but I didn't know where she was.

My phone buzzed, and I answered it. "Yeah."

"We have eyes on the lawyer's car," Jude said. My mind snapped into focus, and I began to move. The cops at the courthouse wanted me to wait and give a statement.

Fuck that.

I wasn't waiting. Every second away from Mara was another second closer to losing her forever, and I wasn't letting that happen.

Her lawyer. They got to her fucking *lawyer*.

"Where?" I was already in motion, ducking past the chaos of people trying to figure out why a lawyer and witness were missing. But they weren't going to find them.

"South on seventeen," Jude said. "Moving fast. Looks like they're going to run into the ten."

The ten, which ran half the way to Mexico. "Daniel," I said.

"We know," Daniel said. "We're going to do everything we can to help you from here. Start driving, and I don't care how many traffic laws you break, I'm already on it. Get to her."

I slid into the driver's seat and gunned the engine. Thankfully, the mechanic, Dave, had left me with a full tank of gas in the new car.

My phone buzzed with a text. "Fuck," I breathed the word.

"What?"

I swallowed, pain in my throat. "It's a text from Mara."

Only one word.

HELP.

"She texted for help." My voice sounded like it had been dragged over broken glass.

"Liam, *drive*," Daniel ordered.

I did. Throwing the car into gear, I burned rubber leaving the parking lot and left honking horns in my wake. As long as I didn't cause any accidents, I wasn't slowing down, and I wasn't stopping for anything.

"What do we know?" I snapped. "Anything on this Neil guy?"

"Yeah," Jude said. "He visited Malcolm a couple of times early on in his prison sentence and never again. We only did a cursory look at those, and nothing popped. Now I think he didn't come back on purpose because he was communicating with Malcolm another way."

In the background, I heard low voices. Everyone was on deck, trying to do whatever they could from half a country away.

"We got a grainy picture, but nothing solid from recently. His appearance has changed. Looks like he's had major surgery. And it looks like he's trying to take Malcolm Novic's place in every sense of the word."

"What?" I shook my head. "He's trying to look like him?"

"Not what we need to focus on. Border Patrol has been notified," Lucas said. "They have a picture of Mara and of Claire. We sent them what we had for Neil."

"It doesn't matter," I ground out. "They're not going through a checkpoint."

Silence came from the other end of the line.

"Thank you," I finally said. "Sorry."

"Don't fucking apologize," Lucas said. "Focus on what's in front of you."

All I could think about was that day in the gym with

Lucas when I'd admitted my deepest fear. The one I was face-to-face with right now. What if I couldn't protect Mara?

I *hadn't* protected her. Something had been off in my gut, and I'd still let her walk away from me. My heart collapsed in on itself. This was my fault. We could have stayed another day, gone to the courthouse, and none of this would have happened.

"You don't know that," Grant said.

Shit. I hadn't realized I'd said it out loud. "I do."

"No," he said. "You don't. Sabotaging the car? They had no way of knowing if you'd actually call Claire. That was one of the plans they had. But they've been *planning* this, Liam. You and I both know you never have only one plan. You have every possible plan. I would bet my entire life savings they had people waiting for you outside the courthouse. They would have dropped you and taken her. You could be lying dead on the asphalt right now."

I took a deep breath. They were right, but it didn't erase the guilt raging in my chest. Mara was *mine*, and I'd let her go. I'd abandoned her, just like everyone in my life had done to me. The spiral of thoughts wouldn't let me go.

Pressing down on the gas, I shot past cars going half my speed. Close the distance. "They're going how fast?"

"Limit," Jude said.

Good. Speed limit meant they were trying *not* to draw attention to themselves. I, on the other hand, didn't care who saw.

God, how could this happen? The lawyer? How did I not see this coming? How could I possibly be worthy of Mara when I hadn't seen what I should have? What if this was the thing that made her realize the truth and leave?

Three taps.

I focused on the memory of her tapping my hand this morning before she left, a confident smile on her face.

How the hell didn't we check deeper? How didn't I *know*?

"Was there any sign of this?" I asked desperately. "With the lawyer. Could we have seen this coming?"

Daniel's voice was grim. "I don't say this often, but I don't think we could have. They were so careful. It's one of the cleanest trails I've ever seen. They learned after Malcolm's arrest—and quickly."

I gritted my teeth and focused on the road. In my life, I'd already lost a woman because I hadn't been enough. Wasn't good enough and hadn't done enough. It wasn't going to happen again. If I lost this time, I would lose having given fucking *everything*.

"Okay, Liam." Daniel's voice came clear through the phone. "We have a plan. But you're going to have to trust us."

Nausea churned in my gut. Trusting them meant I likely wasn't going to like whatever they asked me to do. "Talk to me."

"We're tracking the car. Law enforcement understands the situation. The court has backed us up, and they have your police report from last time. They'll set up blockades wherever they can. But where the car is now, there're too many ways they could branch off. We have to wait until they're locked in to make the call."

"Okay."

It made sense. I didn't like it, but it made sense.

"There's also an accident between you, and traffic is slowing. At this rate, we don't see a way for you to catch up to them."

I swore, and Daniel cut me off. "Catch up to them in the *car*, Liam."

"You have something else in mind?"

"We do," Noah said. "Get ready to fly, brother."

235

Relief flooded my system as my brain shifted into a different kind of mission mode. "What do you have for me?"

"Remember our chase with Emma? Police chopper," Daniel said. "Three more exits. Get off and take a right. Four miles straight west. We'll feed you the rest of the directions as you go."

I wove through traffic, barely clearing the cars I was passing. "What did you tell them? Are they going to hold me back?"

"No," Noah said. "They've been instructed to follow your orders and get you where you need to go. As soon as you get there, you'll have an open line and everything you need."

My heart pounded in my chest, flickering through the many different possibilities. "Parachutes?"

"No."

A chute would take too long anyway. The car wasn't going to stop long enough for me to drift down from the sky. "Guns?"

"Yes," Daniel said. "As many as they have. And I know you're not going to like this, but try to keep the asshole alive."

He was right. I didn't like it. Generally, I liked to think I wasn't a violent person, but this was Mara, and someone else had put their hands on her. "Why." I spat the word. It wasn't a question; it was a demand.

"Because we don't know if he's taken anyone else," Lucas said. "And if there's a chance of saving anyone else, we need to take it."

"That being said…" Daniel was far calmer than I was. "If it's a choice between keeping him alive and saving Mara? You know what to do."

"Damn right," I said.

My phone buzzed.

Liam. I love you.

The words hit me straight in the chest. That was a good-bye. She was preparing me in case she didn't come back. But she was coming back. We were going to have the life we envisioned together, and this was going to *end* for her.

I would try to keep Neil alive, but Mara came first. Speeding off the exit they instructed, I barely slowed down. I didn't care if I had to jump out of the helicopter without a chute, I was getting the woman I loved. One way or another.

Chapter 27

Mara

MUTE.

I was mute.

Every fear I'd ever had came back to life, and my body was frozen in place. No chance of moving, barely breathing, let alone speaking. My phone lay smashed on the ground behind us at the gas station. Neil had ripped it out of my hand and made sure to crush it under his heel before shutting the door and locking it.

Even if I wanted to move, the handcuffs made it difficult.

I didn't see it at first. But the man in the back seat looked like Malcolm. Not enough to be mistaken for him, but he'd clearly had work done to look like the man who haunted my nightmares. It wasn't a good look.

Not that I was going to say it.

He talked like him too. The tone and cadence. He'd studied Malcolm until he was *becoming* him.

It had been nearly an hour of breathless silence. I moved,

and the handcuffs made a grating metallic sound in the silence.

"The handcuffs are only temporary, Mara, I promise. Once you remember the truth, they'll come off. You've been away from the fold too long. But you'll remember. People always remember when they come back."

I swallowed. Of course they "remembered." Because they were trying to avoid whatever beating or consequence was coming to them if they didn't follow his exact instructions.

Digging deep, I pulled in a breath. "Why do you look like Malcolm?"

Neil smiled. "Do you like it? It's not perfect yet, but there's still time. I thought it might ease the transition for The Family to have someone who looked familiar."

"So, they…don't know about this?"

"Some of them do. And soon, they all will. Once we get home and tell them everything, they'll all be with us."

A chill ran down my spine. What could I do? I needed to get out of this, and I had no idea how.

He touched my shoulder from where he sat, and it was all I could do not to recoil. "There are so many of us who have looked forward to your return, Mara. I'd kept the veil and the dress. It's a pity they had to be destroyed to get you back, but we won't be waiting on dresses and veils now. It's been long enough, and The Family can change with the times."

With the times? Because kidnapping women to marry a whole community of men was totally with the times.

"You really did me a favor, Mara, helping put Malcolm away all those years ago. I mean, he helped lay the ground-work, but his leaving was what gave The Family a chance to actually change. Grow. I think you'll be impressed with what we've become."

I doubted that.

"But the biggest reason I have to thank you is for introducing me to Claire. She made so many things happen for us."

Looking over at her, I kept my breath and voice steady. The fear was so strong it was as if I'd removed myself from everything else. "You sent the packages."

"Of course she did." Neil didn't let her speak. "Like a loyal wife should. She'll be one of my wives as well. But you'll be first, Mara. You'll always be first. For everyone."

The statement didn't seem to bother Claire. In fact, she no longer seemed agitated at all. Perfectly calm and happy now that Neil was in the car. A dreamy, contented smile filled her face.

"Where are we going?" If I could keep him talking and keep them both distracted, maybe I could think of something to help me.

Neil sighed and leaned back against the seat. He didn't have a seat belt on from what little I could see in the rearview mirror. "Ecuador. It took everything we had to get people down there and set up the new compound. But this one is much better. Much more secure. Plus, as long as we keep paying the right people, Ecuador has a handy habit of not complying with extradition requests."

"So, everyone is there?" I asked.

"Almost." He shrugged.

Sickness roiled into my stomach. He was basically telling me there was no coming back from this.

I closed my eyes.

Focus, Mara. You are not that girl in the closet.

The last few years, I'd seen my friends and family do incredible things to save the ones they loved. Now it was me. My entire life, I had stayed silent and let things happen. Even now, it was my first instinct to curl up into a ball and hide until everything went away.

That wasn't going to work if I ever wanted to see anyone I loved ever again.

If I ever wanted to see Liam again.

The car flew down the highway. A glance over at the dashboard told me we were going nearly seventy. If I bailed out of the car, I could die. Not ideal. But signs for Mexico were appearing. If I didn't fight before we crossed the border, it would be so much harder.

What would Liam do?

Anything.

Liam would do anything to get to me. It was what he was doing right now. I knew it. And I needed to do anything in order to get back to him.

The car needed to slow down. Though it wasn't busy, the highway was full of enough cars that I didn't want to hurt anyone. But it might be my only option, if it came down to it.

More than anything, I needed Neil to relax and not think I was trying to get away. If they thought I would try to get away at every turn, I would never be able to.

Because of Liam, and the rest of my friends, and also thanks to Rayne, I had my voice back.

Time to use it.

"I couldn't…say anything until now," I said. "But I'm glad we're leaving."

Claire looked over at me, the dreamy smile on her face fading. Likewise, Neil met my eyes in the mirror. "Really?"

"Yeah." My voice came out hoarse. "It's been really hard being away. Harder than I let anyone know. Because people don't understand what it's like to be part of a true family."

I knew exactly what it was like now, and it was the reason

I was able to keep my voice steady as I lied. "It's a relief to be going home for real."

"Then why did you help Malcolm stay in prison?" Claire asked. "You could have said no and not testified."

"I just—" I broke my voice off. "I just needed to see him. When I was overwhelmed at the first hearing, it wasn't because I was afraid. I was just so upset that I couldn't go back in time."

They were still suspicious. "Besides, you seemed happy that he was staying in jail. Isn't it a good thing for all of us?"

In the mirror, Neil grinned. It was the smile of someone so completely out of touch with reality, and *that* was what made it terrifying. "It is a good thing. Malcolm was the past. And we're the future, Mara."

I forced myself to smile. "I'd still like to wear a dress, please. It doesn't have to have all the embroidery, but I still want to look beautiful for you."

"Oh, you will."

The tiny imprint on the dashboard in front of me drew my attention. *Airbags*. This car had airbags, and it might be the thing to save my life.

"Will you take these off?" I lifted my wrists. "I'm happy to be coming home with you. Do I need to be chained up like a criminal?"

Neil chuckled and leaned forward, wrapping a hand around the back of my neck and pressing a hot kiss to my cheek. I nearly gagged. "Not yet, Mara." His words rumbled near my ear.

Don't move. Don't move. Don't move.

"Don't worry, I believe you. And I'll believe you even more when I see you smiling at the end of the aisle. But until then, the cuffs stay on. I can't take the chance you'll be taken from me again." His voice dropped to a sickening whisper. "I've waited too many years to have you."

He leaned back finally, releasing my neck, and I hauled in air, trying to feel less sick. And less nervous about what I was about to do. We were in the right lane, and there was an overpass coming. If I didn't want to hurt anyone else on the road, this was my best chance.

"Okay," I said. "Whatever you need to trust me is fine."

Claire smiled, and in the mirror, Neil checked his phone. For the first time, his eyes weren't glued directly on me. He was distracted and she was relaxed. It had to be now.

Sending a prayer this worked and didn't leave me dead, I took a breath.

Just before the overpass, I lunged, grabbing the steering wheel and yanking it as hard as I could, before Claire could react. We were going too fast, and there was no chance for her to correct our course. She screamed, and I closed my eyes just before we crashed headlong into the bridge.

Chapter 28

Liam

THE CHOPPER WAS LOUD. Even with the headphones on, I found it was an effort to focus my thoughts. The line was open to the guys back home, and I could switch back and forth between them and the local cops as needed.

Right now, we were chasing the car Mara was in, and we were almost there. A few more seconds and I'd have a true visual on her.

"We have the blockade?" I asked.

"They're on it," Lucas called out. "Five minutes till they're done setting it up."

The cars below moved evenly in the flow of traffic. "Any sign they know we're coming?"

"No." Jude's voice came over the line this time. "Everything's the same. They're going a touch slower now, but it seems fine."

Good. That was good.

"You have a plan, Liam?" Noah asked.

"No," I admitted. "Not until we get close enough."

"You're almost there."

Standing, I looked out the front window. We were definitely gaining. It was hard to have a plan when all I wanted to do was lay hands on the man who'd taken Mara. The more likely outcome was that the blockade would stop the car. But I needed a plan anyway.

"Keep telling me how close, please."

"Yeah, we'll keep you updated on—" Daniel's voice cut off midsentence. It wasn't the connection. Everyone at Resting Warrior had gone silent.

"Guys? What's going on?"

An eternity passed in the next seconds before Daniel spoke. "The next overpass, Liam. The car suddenly veered to the right underneath it. Confirming the car did not come out on the other side."

My stomach plummeted through the core of the earth. What were the odds the car had simply pulled over beneath the overpass. But at that speed and a sudden jerk on the wheel? They crashed. Mara had crashed. "Shit. Daniel."

"Don't react before you know, Liam. Get to her. Now."

Noise whooshed in my ears, and I flicked the channel over to the pilot. "Land on the overpass."

"There are cars—"

"The targets just crashed beneath the bridge and might be injured or on foot. Get EMS here now, and *land on the fucking bridge.*"

"Yes, sir."

I flicked the channel back. "We're landing on the overpass. Anything?"

"Nothing. Traffic is stopping, though."

"Shit," I muttered. If traffic was stopping, it confirmed a crash—and probably a bad one. There wasn't time for me to make my way down beneath the bridge the safe way. The good thing about this being a police helicopter was they had everything I needed. Gloves, rope, and guns.

I wasn't taking a gun into this scenario, though. The psychopath probably already had one, and the more guns, the more likely Mara would be injured. The asshole could shoot at me. I would not be shooting anywhere near Mara.

The overpass came underneath us, sirens sounding as cops tried to block off the road and ambulances approached. I slid on gloves as the helicopter descended and focused my mind like I was getting ready for a real jump. I visualized the plan step by step, so all I had to do was execute. Nothing else but the plan. Nothing else.

At least I wasn't jumping out of a helicopter without a chute.

Just off a bridge.

"Wish me luck."

"Liam—"

I ripped off the headset and grabbed the coil of rope beside me and launched myself out the door before the helicopter even touched the ground. Knots. I whipped the rope around the railing and tied it off. Twice. Once more. It was solid, and just as Daniel said, the cars beneath me weren't moving.

It wasn't jumping out of a plane, but it felt the same. There was no time to secure myself. I leaped over the edge of the bridge, letting the gloves take most of the friction and lowered myself to the ground. My arms screamed, palms burning through the gloves.

My feet hit the ground too hard, impact jolting through me. It didn't matter. Mara was all that mattered.

Oh god. The car was destroyed. The entire front end crushed, airbags deployed, and windshield cracked all to hell. I sprinted to the car, praying that Mara was alive. "*Mara!*" I ripped the door open to an empty seat. No one in the back seat either. The only person in the car was Claire, slumped in the driver's seat. Her chest moved up and down, and she had no obvious injuries.

But where was Mara?

Panic crashed down on me. What if she was never in the car and we'd been chasing the wrong target the whole time? What if I'd already lost her?

A scream shattered the air.

Every hair stood on end, because I knew the voice. It was Mara. I'd never heard Mara scream, and I never wanted to hear the sound ever again.

"*Liam!*"

I turned and found her.

Despite everything happening, the world slowed, and pride filled my chest. Mara had found her voice, and she was using it.

She screamed my name again, and everything snapped into focus. Neil was dragging her away, handcuffed, toward the stalled traffic.

I sprinted across the asphalt toward them, only for him to turn, shoving Mara back, and raise the gun toward me. The air moved by me as I dropped to the ground, a bullet coming far too close. Mara was still screaming. Neil stared me down. I tensed, ready to throw myself in either direction to avoid getting shot.

The man smiled. The same insanity that had been in Malcolm's eyes lived in Neil's. Maybe it was the same because they both clung to the same sick ideals. Or maybe Neil was even further gone, trying to become the man he'd been mentored by all those years ago.

He turned away and pointed the gun at the nearest car. "Get out." He bellowed the words so loudly they echoed beneath the bridge. The gun now swung between me and the shaky driver of the car, who got out with her hands raised.

"Mara," I called. "It's going to be fine."

Neil shoved her into the car through the driver's seat and over to the passenger seat. Mara stared at me through the window, tears streaming down her face. The gun was still pointed at me, and I didn't step forward. But I raised my hand to my chest and tapped three times.

Her handcuffed hands pressed against the window, and I ensured the agony in my chest wasn't reflected on my face. She needed strength right now. I would always be that for her.

Neil got behind the wheel and gunned the engine, burning rubber and speeding straight into the empty highway in front of him.

As soon as he cleared me and I wasn't in danger of being shot, my phone was in my hand and dialing. "Follow that car. She and Neil are inside it."

"Blockade is locked and loaded," Daniel said. "A bit far, but they've got cops on the exits too."

I spun, looking around.

"Hey!" a voice yelled at me, a man waving his hand from the front row of cars. He gestured to me, and I ran. "That your girl?"

"Yes."

"Take the car."

I didn't hesitate or question him. "Thank you."

Flipping the phone to speaker, I tossed it on the passenger seat. "I have a vehicle, and I'm in pursuit."

My heart was calm now, because I knew something Neil didn't know.

Mara and I were part of a family, too. And they would do anything for us. Not because they were forced to, or brainwashed. But because they loved us. The men on the other end of the line were just as much on the edge of their seat as I was.

No matter the planning he'd done for this day, no matter how many surgeries he'd had to make himself look like Malcolm, and no matter what sacrifices he'd made for this win…he'd already lost.

I gunned the engine, taking off after the car. They were heading directly into a blockade. There was nowhere for him to go, and I wanted to make sure he couldn't go backward either.

"Daniel," I called. "They know she's in the car?"

"Police?"

"Yeah."

"They know."

I took a breath. "Tell them again, please. Make sure."

He didn't question it. They were driving straight into a mess of police cars and guns. If there were bullets involved, they needed to be aimed at the tires and nowhere else.

"How far out are they?" A faint murmur of voices was audible on the end of the line. "How far, guys?"

"Three minutes. Everything's set."

"Okay," I said and pushed down the pedal, flooring it. "Let's do this."

I'm coming, Mara.

Chapter 29

Mara

HE WAS HERE. Liam was *here*.

Somewhere behind this car, he was coming after me.

He'd tapped his heart three times. It was all I needed to see. I swiped away the tears on my face. They were a reaction I couldn't stop, my body knowing the fear that my mind held at bay.

I leaned away from Neil as far as I could, keeping my body facing him. Gone was the man who tried to be charming and told me he wanted me. As much as I hated that version of Neil, I preferred it to this one.

This Neil tapped the gun against his thigh, looking behind us. "You lied to me, Mara. You told me you wanted to come with me, and then you crashed the car. *You* crashed the car. *You* showed everyone where we fucking were."

He looked behind us again, and I turned.

The road was empty. For now.

I didn't respond to his words. What would I say? It was true. I'd lied. I didn't ever want to go with him.

"Him?" he asked. "He is who you choose over The Family who raised you? The Family who gave you *everything*?"

New fear took root. Neil was still tapping the gun.

"You did this, Mara. I knew it might happen, but I hoped it wouldn't. But no one ever leaves The Family. You know that. Even in death."

My breath stilled in my chest. He would kill us both before letting us be taken. That was always the backup plan. Take me back to the compound, or kill me and make sure I died a bride of honor.

"You could get away," I said. "Right now. Pull over and run. There's no one in sight, and I won't say anything. All I want is to go home, Neil. Not to The Family. *Home*. And you can go home too."

He snarled—a sound that should never come from a human. "And what kind of leader does that make me? A coward. Besides, they'll all know once we're gone. If we don't make it, they'll know it was because of you."

In the side mirror, a car appeared behind us. My heart leaped into my throat. It was just the one car, and there was only one person who would be chasing us.

Liam.

Neil noticed at the same time.

Ahead of us in the distance, I saw flashing lights. So many flashing lights. Police all across the road, spread out. They were going to puncture the tires and make us stop. Relief and terror lived side by side within me.

"I'm not Malcolm, Mara. I will not spend my life in prison. Nor am I a coward. I am the leader of The Family, and they will remember me doing whatever I had to do to bring back someone who was lost. The Family will go on without us, and we'll meet everyone else we've lost on the other side."

He didn't slow down. We hurtled toward the blockade of police at full speed, and I saw guns pointed at us. Liam would never let them shoot at me. But Neil would shoot me. Before, I'd worried about getting run over by another car or causing an accident. Now, I had none of that to consider. Risking my life was a better option than getting shot in the head.

And Neil hadn't locked the doors on this car.

Neil looked over at me and smiled. "I loved you, you know. All this time, I saw you for what you were and knew that when we were finally together, it would be beautiful. I'm sorry it can't be in this life. But we'll be together forever now."

The gun no longer tapped against his leg. He held it steady. And it rose in my direction.

I didn't think. For the second time in a vehicle today, I lunged. Tucking myself into a ball, I pulled on the door handle and *launched* myself from the car.

Pain ripped into me, the impact throwing me and rolling me. Never in my life had I felt this kind of pain. Not even when Malcolm was beating me. But if I was in pain, I was alive.

I was alive.

Through the darkness and pulsing agony, I heard tires ripping open and the sound of gunshots. Squealing and sliding. Pressure.

"Mara."

Were those sirens?

"Thank god," I heard in a low whisper. "Hang on, sweetheart. Help is coming."

That was Liam's voice. Liam.

I loved him.

That comfort took me down into the dark.

———

SLOW, methodical beeping echoed in my brain. Too soft to be an alarm, too slow to be a siren. Was the smoke alarm going off? What the hell was it?

I opened my eyes and found a white drop ceiling above me. Where the hell was I?

And—

Oh *fuck*.

Everything hurt.

"Ow."

The one syllable was wholly inadequate.

"Mara?"

I couldn't move my head, but it didn't matter. Liam's face appeared over mine. Everything came back in a painful, colorful flurry. But I was *alive*.

He leaned down and kissed me. Gently. I wanted so much more—I wanted to consume him, because where Liam was, there was no pain.

"Where are we?"

"The hospital," Liam said. "Making sure you're okay."

I blinked. "How long has it been?"

He sighed. "A day. You jumped out of the car yesterday."

"A day…"

Liam's forehead pressed against mine. "Yes, sweetheart. God, I want to pull you into my arms right now, but I don't want to hurt you. I love you. I love you so much."

He kissed me again, and I relaxed. We were here together, and we were safe. "You got my text?"

"I did." Pain filled his eyes. "I'm so sorry you thought you had to say goodbye. I never should have let you walk away from me."

"You didn't know."

Knuckles stroked my cheek. "That doesn't matter."

"I love you," I whispered. The first time I'd spoken the words aloud. "I wasn't saying goodbye. I just wanted to make sure I said it in words and not tapping."

"I heard you, sweetheart. Loud and clear. I am so fucking proud of you, though I never want to hear you scream again."

I laughed and then groaned. The motion hurt too. "Hopefully I won't have to. How bad is the damage?"

"Broken arm," Liam said. "The rest is some big-time bruising and scrapes. Along with feeling like you got hit by a truck, because hitting asphalt at that speed *is* kind of like getting hit by a truck. But you got lucky."

His voice told me everything I needed to know about how terrified he'd been. "Why can't I move my head?"

"Neck brace as a precaution. Now that you're awake, we'll have the doctors come by, and hopefully you can take it off." He took my hand gently, squeezing. Nothing between our hands, so no cast on my right. Left must be broken.

"What happened? Is Neil—"

"Dead. It all happened fast. He hit the spike strip and came out shooting. The police took him down before he even took a step. And Malcolm… Well, he's dead too. Someone in the prison."

Sweet relief and freedom filled my chest. "I shouldn't be happy to hear that," I said. "But I am."

He grinned. "I won't tell anyone. But I am too. There's more to tell you, though. Claire is alive and has been arrested. He did a number on her and her mind. But there's no question about whether she's going to jail."

"I'm not testifying," I said immediately.

"You don't have to. There's plenty of evidence against her already. And Brynn is here in the hospital as well."

I blinked. "What?"

Liam told me his side of the story, from the water in the gas tank to being approached by Brynn. And everything that came after.

"I guess you were right," I said quietly. "About her showing up at exactly the right time."

"Maybe. But she helped save your life. She snapped out of it and knows what she did. If anything, it's impressive. And seeing her the way she was…" He sighed. "He messed with her mind. She didn't know any better. But now, I think she has a chance."

"Did Claire say anything about Ecuador?"

Liam frowned. "Not that I know of. Why?"

"It's where the new compound is," I said. "He told me in the car."

"I know a few people who will be very interested in that piece of information," Liam said quietly, though he was brushing his lips over my skin.

"Everyone back home?"

His grin lit up the whole room. "Going crazy to talk to you as soon as you'll let them."

I smiled. "Maybe in a little while." While I loved our family, they were also overwhelming, and I wasn't sure I could take the kinds of questions and phone passing that would happen on a call. As it was, as soon as we got home, I knew everyone would be falling over themselves to help.

"You got it."

"Our patient is awake, I see." A man in a white coat stood in the doorway. "Nice to officially meet you."

"Hi," I said, my voice sounding more like a croak than anything else.

"I'm Dr. Araya. I've been looking after you since you were brought in."

"Can she take the brace off?" Liam asked.

"X-rays didn't show any damage to the spinal column. And now that you're awake and can tell us if you're in pain, you can take it off."

He helped me, gently undoing the Velcro closure and pulling it out from behind my head. I slowly turned my head from side to side and then moved it up and down. "It feels fine. Which seems like a miracle."

"Honestly?" The doctor laughed. "It is. You could have ended up with much, much worse."

"Yeah…" I looked at him. "How long do I have to stay?"

He marked something down on my chart before hanging it on the end of the bed again. "I'd like you to stay a couple more days just in case. With incidents like these, sometimes there are deeper things which don't reveal themselves right away. But I promise, we'll get you out of here as soon as possible."

I nodded. "Could I go see someone?" In the corner of my eye, I saw Liam's brows rise. "She's here in the hospital."

"I'll allow it," Dr. Araya said. "But wheelchair only."

"Thank you."

He smiled at us both. "I'll check on you again in a bit before I go home for the night."

I looked over at Liam, who took my hand in both of his. "You want to see Brynn?"

"Yeah. I feel like I need to."

"Let me go grab you a wheelchair."

As he left, I moved a little more, testing my boundaries. It hurt, but not as much as when I'd first woken. Liam was right. Mostly bruising. I could move. And I took the opportunity to slowly sit up and shift myself off the bed, taking my IV with me as I shuffled to the bathroom. I loved the man, but we weren't at the point where I wanted him to help me pee.

He entered the room with a wheelchair right as I exited

the bathroom, and he scrubbed a hand over his face. "I am so glad I didn't walk in ten seconds ago and think you'd disappeared again."

I walked over to him and wrapped my arms around him, awkward with the cast. It would take both of us a while to get over that. "I'm not going anywhere," I said. "I'm moving in, remember?"

Liam squeezed tighter. "Oh, I remember, sweetheart. I can't wait."

We got a little carried away kissing before I remembered I was supposed to be sitting down in the wheelchair. "Let's go."

He looked me up and down. "You sure?"

"As much as I'd like to stay here and do *that*, I'd rather not while in the hospital."

"That's fair," he muttered. "I'll just die quietly."

I smacked his arm and sat in the chair while he took me to Brynn's room. It wasn't far from mine. "Do you want me with you?" he asked.

"No," I said and leaned my head on his arm. "I think this has to be me."

Leaning down, Liam kissed the top of my head. "I'll be right outside if you need me."

The maneuvering was more difficult with a cast, but I managed. Her eyes locked on mine the second I turned the corner, and whatever I'd thought to say flew right out of my head. Liam was right. She had been beaten so badly it was amazing she'd even made it to Liam in the first place.

"I'm so sorry," she whispered.

I rolled closer. "Liam told me you helped save my life. I came to say thank you."

Brynn stared. "You're not angry with me?"

"I thought I might be," I admitted, looking away. "But how can I be, when I've been there? It took me until *now* to be able to speak regularly again. What they did to our minds goes deep. You didn't hurt me, and you helped save my life. I can't be angry with you for falling under the same spell as everyone who believed them."

Silence stretched between us, Brynn looking down at her hands. "I'm still sorry, Mara. I'm…so ashamed I believed all of it. It seems so stupid now. How could I fall for something like that? And what do I do now?"

I shrugged. "You find a way through it, and you're already Rayne's client. Even if everything you were telling her was fake."

She laughed, but there was no humor in it. "I guess I could go back to Montana. But I don't have anyone there. I don't have anyone anywhere now."

The people at Resting Warrior wouldn't hold this against her. I would make sure of it. Because programming like ours went so deep, you couldn't fight it, and she had a hell of a journey in front of her.

"Well," I said. "It's a good thing you know a place that specializes in helping people heal from trauma."

Brynn's mouth opened and closed. "They would help me? After what I did?"

"Liam?" I called. He stepped into the doorway immediately. "Would Resting Warrior have a place for Brynn?"

He thought about it. "I'll have to talk to Daniel, but I don't see why not."

Tears filled her eyes. "Thank you."

"Just focus on getting better," Liam said. "Once you're out of the hospital, we'll talk about it."

She seemed so overwhelmed, we took our leave, going back to my room. "Do you think you'll get in trouble if you get in bed with me?"

"It's worth the risk." Liam didn't hesitate to kick off his

shoes and help me into the bed before sliding in behind me and wrapping an arm around me.

I would never take this feeling for granted again. Happiness and safety. Comfort and love. We were going home. This time, forever.

"I love you," I said quietly.

Liam tapped my hand three times.

Epilogue

Mara - Three months later

SNOW FELL OUTSIDE THE WINDOWS, and I snuggled deeper into the blankets next to Liam. A fire roared in the fireplace, and I still wanted all the heat. Maybe it was all the time I'd spent in Arizona while I was younger. I loved the cold weather, but I still wanted to soak up heat like a snake on a rock.

The fire crackled merrily in the background, and Liam and I were almost asleep.

I watched the snow whirl outside. "Do you think I should check on Brynn?"

"Why?" I guessed he was further from sleep than I thought. His voice was entirely alert.

"Probably isn't used to snow." It was the first *big* snow of the year. One that might take a few days for Garnet Bend to dig themselves out of. Brynn now lived in the cabin I'd vacated when I moved in with Liam. It was warm, and I wasn't worried about her freezing. But my first snow had been disconcerting too.

"I'll check on her tomorrow," I said.

"Good idea." Liam grabbed me around the waist and rolled, pinning me beneath him on the couch. "I don't want to let you go right now."

"Oh? Sounds like you're starting to get needy," I teased.

He called my bluff, kissing me hard enough we got lost in each other. Home was our favorite place to be. Liam had taken me paragliding one more time after I got my cast off and before it was too cold. We'd also gone camping at the other Resting Warrior property. But we were happiest here, in the place we worked to make a reflection of both of us.

Here, neither of us had to hide who we were. If I was having a bad day with memories or flashbacks, Liam didn't mind if I was silent. Likewise with the memories of his childhood or his injuries. We *worked*. And I was only a little sad we'd waited so long to come together.

Everything happened for a reason. Who knew if anything had happened between us earlier if it would have worked out in the same way? Maybe neither of us would be here.

"I was going to wait until Christmas," Liam said. "But I'm impatient. I can't."

"I can wait for my presents," I told him. "I promise I was teasing." Last week, I'd pouted when he told me he hid the presents.

"This isn't a present. Or at least, it's not the traditional kind."

"Okay…" I drew out the word. "Do I need to sit up for this?"

Liam rested himself more firmly on top of me, settling his hips between my thighs. "No, this is pretty much perfect."

I narrowed my eyes and rocked my hips. "If this is what you mean by a gift, we're *definitely* not waiting for Christmas."

"Mara," he laughed.

Kissing him, I imitated zipping my lips closed and throwing away the key.

"From the first moment I saw you in those flower beds near the Ravali cabin, something in me knew you were special. It may sound crazy, but I think the deepest part of me knew you were going to change my life. I didn't listen, and it took me forever to get my head on straight."

"Happened at a good time, though," I said. "Right when I needed you."

Liam kissed me, his mouth hot and hungry against mine. I slid my hands under his shirt, lifting it up and over his head and tossing it aside. "I'm never going to get through this if you keep doing that," he murmured against my lips.

"Maybe that's my plan. To derail you and make you take me upstairs."

"I promise it's worth it. And when I'm done, I don't have any doubts we'll be upstairs and in bed within five minutes."

I raised an eyebrow. "Intriguing."

"Fuck." He was trying not to laugh and just barely managed to straighten out his expression. "As I was *saying*. It took me a while to get to where I needed to be. Thoughts I wasn't even aware of were holding me back. Thinking I wasn't worthy of you, or of anyone, if I'd been abandoned so many times before. Fear of messing it up and ending up alone again. Worry about what you really thought of me or what everyone else would think."

This time, I didn't interrupt him. I wrapped my arms around his neck, holding him closer. He spoke the next words brushing the skin of my neck. "And I still have those thoughts. That I'm not worthy of you. That I don't deserve you. Someday, I'll do something, and you'll leave."

I knew. We talked about it when he was feeling it, and he was working on the impulses with Rayne.

"But it's getting better," he said.

"Good."

Liam smiled. "That being said, you, Mara Greene, are incredible. You're a survivor. Raised in hell, and when you got out, you didn't curl up into a ball and give up. You made a life for yourself. You kept going until you found a place you could truly heal."

"I didn't heal until you," I told him. "Not really."

Another discussion we'd had. A playful disagreement. I was better, and that was all that mattered. The look on his face told me he knew it too.

"You are beautiful, giving, and kind. You're generous and warm. You are loving. You are resilient. You are *everything* the world tried to take away from you."

Emotion built in my chest. "Liam."

"But most importantly," he said, "you are my home. More than a house or a place, more than everything. Wherever you are, that's where I want to be."

His face blurred in front of me, and I blinked back the tears, wanting to see him clearly.

"I know we're not normal," he said with a grin. "We both come from pasts with shit that would break other people. And I know, too, that because of them" —we never said "The Family" anymore— "and because of what they did and used against you, marriage may not be something you want."

I shuddered involuntarily. No. It wasn't. I understood the beauty of a real marriage and everything it stood for. Still, every time I imagined walking down an aisle toward someone—even Liam—my mind was thrown back into pure panic. It didn't matter if I wanted it, they'd ruined that for me. One thing I wasn't sure I'd ever reclaim.

"And that's fine with me," Liam said. "My marriage did a number on me, too. It doesn't bother me not to have the piece of paper."

"But?" I asked. This was clearly leading somewhere.

"But—" he finally moved, pulling us up into a sitting position on the couch "—I wanted to ask you two things."

Tossing the blanket we'd been snuggled under to the side, he knelt in front of me. I stared at him, suddenly apprehensive.

"Mara Greene, I love you. I am so in love with you, it sometimes hurts to breathe. Everything I told you the first night I admitted it is still true. I envision waking up with you every day for the rest of my life. You make me so happy, and I don't ever want to let you go.

"So…" He smiled. "I'm not asking you to marry me. But I am asking you to be mine forever. Promise me that we're in this for good. Share this life with me. Have babies with me. Fight with me. Fuck with me. Be my partner and my safe place. And I will be all of those things for you. I'd even help carry the babies if I could."

I choked out a laugh, stifled by the tears running down my face.

Liam's eyes shone too, and he took both of my hands in his. "What do you say?"

"Yes." The word was half sob, half joy, and I fell to my knees with him, kissing him until I couldn't breathe. "I mean, I thought we were already doing it, but *yes*."

He laughed into my mouth. "I wanted to make sure. And I wanted to propose anyway, despite not getting married."

"It was perfect." He'd said he had a two-part question. "What was the other thing you were going to ask?"

He chuckled and went over to the tree and pulled out a tiny box hidden in the branches. "Well, it's a twofold question. The first part is if you would mind if I wore a ring? I want everyone to know I'm yours."

When he opened the box, a plain silver band was inside. Clearly for him. I examined the thoughts going through my head. Would it bother me? No. It wouldn't. It was the wedding and the *marriage* that bothered me. Being a bride and a wife, because of everything it had come to mean.

Seeing Liam wear a ring to represent our commitment? I liked it. A lot. "I like that idea."

"Yeah?"

"Yeah." I took the ring out of the box and slipped it on his finger. The silver stood out against his dark skin, and I *loved* seeing it there.

"The second part of the question is, do you want one too? There's no pressure to say yes, sweetheart, and I won't be offended if you say no. I just wanted to ask."

"Do you have one?" I asked.

He smirked. "No. Not yet. I didn't want you to feel stressed if you saw the real thing."

The idea of wearing a ring on my finger was treading into dangerous territory. Eventually, I thought I could do it. "Would it bother you if I wanted to wear the ring on a necklace and work up to it?"

"Not at all." He leaned in and kissed my neck. "I'll like watching it swing when you're on top of me."

I laughed. "You're insatiable."

"When it comes to you? Yes."

"Then, yes," I told him. "I want a ring. Hopefully someday, I'll be able to wear it for real."

Liam stood and pulled me with him, lifting me into his arms and heading for the stairs. "Even if you never do, Mara, I'll love that you have it. I'm going to love picking it out too. With your help."

He carried me into our bedroom, not bothering to turn

on the light. We sprawled on our bed together, Liam bracing himself over me. "But right now, I'm going to enjoy this. Wearing my ring. Knowing I'll never belong to anyone else but you."

"I love you." I pulled him down to kiss me. "I'm yours. Forever."

Also by Josie Jade

See more info here: www.josiejade.com

RESTING WARRIOR RANCH (with Janie Crouch)

Montana Sanctuary

Montana Danger

Montana Desire

Montana Mystery

Montana Storm

Montana Freedom

Montana Silence

Montana Rain

About the Author

Josie Jade is the pen name of an avid romantic suspense reader who had so many stories bubbling up inside her she had to write them!

Her passion is protective heroes and books about healing…broken men and women who find love—and themselves—again.

Two truths and a lie:
- Josie lives in the mountains of Montana with her husband and three dogs, and is out skiing as much as possible
- Josie loves chocolate of all kinds—from deep & dark to painfully sweet
- Josie worked for years as an elementary school teacher before finally becoming a full time author

Josie's books will always be about fighting danger and standing shoulder-to-shoulder with the family you've chosen and the people you love.

Heroes exist. Let a Josie Jade book prove it to you.

Printed in the USA
CPSIA information can be obtained
at www.ICGtesting.com
LVHW091142130524
779900LV00005B/646

9 781950 802722